ATLAS 5

A DISASTER THRILLER

JIM LESTER

Atlas 5

Print ISBN 979-8-35091-024-7

eBook ISBN 979-8-35091-025-4

CHAPTER 1

2018

HELL IS THE HOTTEST PLACE in the universe. Except for Bay St. Edwards, Florida. There is absolutely no spot in the galaxy hotter and more humid than Bay St. Edwards. Especially in the summertime. And there is no hotter place in Bay St. Edwards than the monkey house at the local zoo, which is where I found myself arguing with my grown daughter as sweat poured down my face in tiny rivers.

"You're the worst grandfather on the planet." Susan was always full of bluster and exaggeration.

"I went to Rand's first football game last fall," I said in a lame effort to defend myself.

"And you looked like a complete jerk." Susan wasn't going to let me off the hook.

"It wasn't that bad."

"You laughed at him. The other parents heard you."

The heat and the stink of monkeys closed in on me like a suffocating blanket and outside, swirling storm clouds were massing and making me nervous. It was not the time to go more rounds with my daughter.

"It was funny," I said. I knew I shouldn't have laughed, but for much of my life, football had almost been like a religion and Rand didn't even like the game. He was much more into computers and video games. "He tripped on his own feet and had to be carried off the field before the game started."

"You know he's always been clumsy." Susan never found much of anything funny.

"He was being a drama king," I said. "He wasn't hurt."

Susan scowled.

"He's a sweet kid," I said. "He's just into his own stuff."

"Hurry up, you guys. It's time for ice cream." Rand, now fourteen and no longer a football wannabe although still a stocky boy, motioned to Susan and me from the monkey house entrance, saving me from further unpleasantness with my daughter. At least for the time being.

When we got outside, the heat and humidity attacked me like a mortar barrage. The storm clouds had a purplish tinge and hovered directly over us.

"Don't say anything, Dad," Susan said. "This is Florida. It's hot in Florida. You'll get used to it. You've only been here a few months. You'll adjust. You're not in Colorado anymore, Toto," Susan said, delighting in my discomfort.

She was right about that. I missed Colorado. I missed the snow and the skiing and the hiking and the frosty mornings. I missed the Broncos. I missed teaching my classes. But my exile in Bay St. Edwards was my own fault. One stupid act. One moment of bad judgment had changed my whole life.

"Oh, come on," I said. "Even you would have to admit it's hot today. And what's wrong with those clouds? I've never seen anything like that."

"Bugs is right," Rand said. "Those are the weirdest clouds ever."

My real name was John Coffman and when the grandchildren were born, I assumed they would call me something like Grandpa or Grandad, or, God forbid, Goompa. But none of that happened. Rand had insisted on calling me "Bugs" since he was a toddler. It had something to do with my white hair that tended to stick out at odd angles, which reminded Rand of a bug and I was stuck with the name.

"I think we're in for a big storm," Rand said. "Lots of humidity, weeks of heavy rain concentrated in the air."

"Maybe some rain would cool things off," I said.

Rand whipped out his smartphone and swiped and punched. He stared at the screen through thick glasses, pushing back a lock of his stringy, blond hair. "Yep. There's a hurricane watch for the whole Emerald Coast. But there seems to be a lot of other crazy stuff happening." Rand never looked up from the little screen.

"What does that mean?"

"A watch means a hurricane is possible in 36 hours," Susan said. She dug her own phone out of the big black bag where she carried all of her real estate salesperson gear. She punched and swiped and shoved the screen in my face. "See."

This was new form of communication in the 21st century. An individual located a photograph or a chart on their phone and then, with a flick of the wrist, they shoved the screen in another person's face. It was irritating as hell.

Susan thrust a weather chart in my face, but the cataracts in my right eye had gotten so bad the whole thing might as well have been in Chinese.

"We get lots of storm watches down here," Susan said. "They usually don't mean anything. The storms in the Gulf either run out of steam or change directions."

"Good to know."

The huge trees on the zoo grounds swayed as the wind whooshed through the leaves. The sky was a gunmetal gray.

Susan smiled that unique smile of hers. The one that denoted absolutely no mirth or joy whatsoever. She was a tall woman, whose height was amplified by her ramrod straight posture. She was always meticulously dressed. Today, she wore a starched white blouse and black slacks.

I loved Susan and deeply regretted how my relationship with my daughter and the kids had worked out since I arrived in Florida. It was my fault. I had been sullen and grumpy since the day I stepped off the plane.

My maroon golf shirt and Rand's unfortunate gray T-shirt with "Too Big to Fail" embossed on the front were soaked with sweat but Susan looked cool and dry. Her dark hair was neatly twisted into a knot on the top of her head, a trendy style that makes me think the women who utilized it should be designated "Knot Heads."

Since we had established that the weather was no big deal, we purchased ice cream cones from a concession stand and found seats at a picnic table under an orange awning that was swaying in the wind.

The faint scent of the monkey house lingered in the humid air.

I attacked my chocolate cone, licking furiously because the ice cream was rapidly turning into a gooey river that ran down my hand. A splotch of chocolate plopped on my shirtfront. Another one landed on my khaki slacks.

"Dad!" Susan scolded. "Watch out. You're going to look like a sloppy old geezer."

I shot Susan what I hoped would be a withering look. "And I should care, why?"

And why should I care? Old men are invisible anyway. Young women look right through them and young men don't even bother to size them up to see if they could take them in a fight. Nobody would notice a little spot on my shirt-front. The actuary tables didn't leave me much time on the planet anyway, so who cared about a couple of spots on my shirt-front?

The wind picked up again, blowing the napkins off of our picnic table and across the grassy space in front of the monkey house.

"For God's sake, Dad. You're not even trying to become a successful old person."

Rand looked away.

"How the hell do you become a successful old person?" More ice cream plopped on my shirtfront.

"I'll tell you how," Susan said. "You take responsibility. You don't hide behind being old. That's what wrong with America today. Nobody takes responsibility. The government tells everybody what to do."

"Oh, come on, Susan. This isn't the time or the place to. . ."

"Everyone has a 'disease.'" Susan made quotation marks in the air with her fingers. "No one is sad. They have 'clinical depression.' No one is a pig. They have an 'eating disorder.'"

We both involuntarily looked at Rand and then quickly looked away.

"No one is shy. They have a 'social avoidance disorder.'"

"I get the picture, Susan. No more please."

"If you have a 'disease.'" The quotation marks again. "Then you're not responsible for your behavior. You can't help yourself. Don't let 'aging' become your 'disease', Dad. It won't work with me."

"Here comes Skylar." Rand had developed an intuitive ability to cut off the simmering hostilities between his mother and me.

Skylar Coffman-Rhodes was my granddaughter. Two years younger than Rand, she was a talented artist, a skilled soccer player and the top student in her sixth-grade class.

"Hi everybody," Skylar sang between loud smacks on a wad of pink gum as she joined us at the picnic table. "The tour was soooo cool. The zookeeper is a total riot."

We had dropped off Skylar earlier for a special zookeeper tour. "The zookeeper really was a hoot," she said. "The woman had a large neck tattoo that looked like an iguana crawling out of her khaki zookeeper's uniform."

She also had a metallic bugger connecting her nostrils. Of all the bizarre youthful fashion trends of recent years, the metallic bugger won my award for the single most hideous decoration a young woman could add to her otherwise pretty face.

Can you imagine Elizabeth Taylor or Marilyn Monroe with a big silver thing hanging out of their nose? Me either.

The wind picked up again and the clouds begin swirling. I felt a gnawing sense of anxiety in my gut.

"That's great, sweetheart," I said. "Tell us about the animals you saw."

Susan disappeared into her cellphone.

Skylar started telling us about a pair of tigers and Susan moved away from the picnic table so she could talk on her cellphone. Susan sold real estate in Bay St. Edwards and every call she got might as well have been from the red phone in Moscow.

"Why does the sky look so funny?" Skylar did a 360 spin as she looked upward.

"There's a hurricane watch," Rand said. "But you're right. I've never seen clouds like that. They're really scary looking."

Skylar shrugged and looked at me. "The zookeeper can make her face look just like the animals she's talking about. It's really cool. And she smelled just like Daddy."

'Daddy' was Susan's ex-husband, Roger and what he smelled like was booze. He had been an okay fellow, but he had been a push-over for Susan. He was a CPA who lacked my daughter's driving ambition. The last thing I'd heard about Roger was that was living in Miami with a younger woman and was happy as a clam.

The wind lashed the zoo. Thick raindrops plunked on the picnic table.

"Come on, guys. We have to go now." Susan dropped her phone in her purse. "I've got a buyer down in Warwick Harbor who is dying to see the Cromwell mansion. I'm supposed to meet him there this afternoon. Hustle up, now or we'll get soaked."

"But I didn't get any ice cream," Skylar said.

"You can get some next time." Susan hoisted her bag over her shoulder like she was about to attack the summit of Mount Everest. Her sleeve rode up, revealing the "Live Free" tattoo on her forearm.

"I'll get her a small cone and she can eat it in the car," I said.

"Dad." Susan looked exasperated. "No. She'll drip it all over the upholstery. Come on everybody. Let's get a move on. I've got important clients waiting."

Actually, a little ice cream wouldn't do much damage to my car. I drove a twelve-year old maroon Lincoln Town Car. It was bigger that a battleship and embarrassed the hell out of Susan. But it was spacious and comfortable. It was a fun car. The kids and I loved it.

I stood up and took a couple of halting steps. My right hip always stiffened if I sat too long and pain shot down my leg. I needed hip replacement surgery, but I kept putting it off.

The swirling clouds grew darker. I didn't care if I was a newcomer to Florida. Something was seriously off in the heavens.

CHAPTER 2

SUSAN AND I HAD BEEN disappointing each other for years. When she was growing up back in Colorado she had been a high achieving, straight A student but when the time came to go to college rolled around, my salary as a high school history teacher ruled out Stanford or Wellesley, Susan's top choices. She eventually graduated from the University of Colorado with honors, but she never let me forget how I didn't earn enough money to send her to a top college.

After college, she joined a string of increasingly nutty far right organizations—liberty and freedom, limited government, defend the second amendment or die. I was an unwavering Bobby Kennedy liberal and our political arguments were the equal of the Ali-Frazier bouts.

Then Susan met Roger and they landed in northern Florida. Even after all our verbal battles, I missed her and wished she lived closer to home.

When everything in my life blew up and I had to get out of Colorado in a hurry, Susan invited me to come and live in Bay St. Edwards. I didn't have a lot of choices. But I treasured my independence and, not wanting to be a burden, I refused to move into the house with Susan and the kids. She grudgingly found me a cheap beach house that was in foreclosure, but after a couple of months, I figured out that my daughter wanted to take advantage of my misfortune and invited me to Florida to serve as a built-in babysitter for Rand and Skylar while she peddled real estate and devoted her spare time to Libertarian causes.

Being a cranky old man, there were a lot of days I didn't feel like being Bugs. I wanted to be left alone, which pissed off Susan to the nth degree. She finally hired Maria, a Cuban housekeeper and babysitter to help with the kids while Susan set about to stop the tide of the evil federal government and assure the supremacy of free market capitalism. Susan was furious with me. If you don't show up to babysit every day, you're the worst grandfather on the planet.

Disappointment and anger abounded on both sides and the trip to the zoo was an effort at a truce.

The wind picked up and I had to grip the steering wheel hard with both hands to keep from being blown onto the other side of the road. This could not be normal.

On the drive back to Susan's house, the kids squabbled about the merits of some hip-hop outfit called Hangnail and Susan hunched over in the passenger seat, swiping and punching her cellphone, occasionally mumbling "shit" under her breath.

I drove north, away from the Gulf and circled through downtown Bay St. Edwards, which consisted of a strip of two-story office buildings, a couple of sea food restaurants, a couple of bars, an art center and a quaint coffee shop. The downtown backed up to the majestic waters of Zephyr Bay. We were at the opposite end of the state from Miami, 630 miles apart, which suited me fine. I'd had all the big city I wanted.

As we headed west down Florida Avenue, the wind blew paper cups, napkins and trash across the road and the sky grew darker.

Family matters are always the most complicated, the most complex and the most vexing. As I entered the fourth quarter of my life, I realized that I had made a mess of my relationships with my entire family, my wife, my daughter, even my grandchildren.

I regretted all of it. Things could have been so different between Susan and me. I mean it didn't have to work out like it did. But maybe someday, in a parallel universe. . .

Susan looked out of her window. "Burger King." She read the sign as we drove past the fast food emporium. When Susan got bored or irritated, she read signs out loud. It was not an endearing trait.

"I'm cold. Can you turn down the air?" Rand called from the back seat.

I complied with his request.

Brightly colored summerhouses lined the road. We drove by a rococo hotel that fronted the white sandy beaches and turquoise waters of Zephyr Bay.

"Bob's Boats and Bait," Susan said a minute later.

"Give it a rest, Susan."

"What's wrong with you, Dad? You don't like anything anymore."

"I like plenty of things," I said. "But this new world is full of stuff I could do without."

"Like what, Bugs?" Rand called from the back seat.

I knew he was baiting me but I couldn't resist. "Like man-buns and man-hugs. What the hell happened to a manly handshake? And stupid end zone dances in a football game. I could definitely live without those silly things. And as far as I'm concerned when you tell me someone tweeted, I assume they passed gas."

"Whoa, Bugs," Rand laughed. "You're gonna give grumpy old men a bad name."

I let out a good-natured snarl.

"Smiling Pooch Dog Kennel."

I reached for the radio.

"Summer Heaven Resort Hotel."

My radio dial was set on an oldies station and the sound of the Monkees' "Last Train to Clarksville" filled the car.

"Groovy, Bugs," Skylar said.

"You guys must have been hard up for music back then," Rand said.

"Rosco's Bar and Grill. Crab Cakes Our Specialty."

"We didn't have a lot of choices back in the Roman Empire," I said to Rand. "This was the best we could do."

"Turn that crap down, Dad!" Susan snapped. "It's way too loud. You're getting hard of hearing. We're all starting to shout when we talk to you. It's embarrassing."

I flicked the dial and the Monkees faded away. Raindrops peppered the windshield and the ancient wipers struggled to keep up.

Susan was right about my hearing. A couple of weeks ago I was in a fast food place and I ordered a bowl of soup and a salad. A perky young woman punched my order into her computer, looked up at me and said, "Would you like a quickie for 99 cents?"

"What?"

"A quickie. For 99 cents."

I looked at the rack of bakery goods behind her. A cookie. Did I want a cookie for 99 cents?

Aging was the pits.

"The Emerald Fields Mall." Susan stared out the window.

The wind and rain lashed the windshield. The humidity soared and sweat trickled down my ribcage.

Susan and the kids lived in the Emerald Fields Estates, which was only a mile from the mall. The house was a Florida ranch style dwelling—a pink stucco with palm trees in the front yard.

My daughter's cellphone went off as I pulled into the driveway.

"Call Sid," Susan said into the phone. "I don't have time today. Honestly. Now listen. Here's what I want you to do." She leaped out of the car and sprinted toward the house, talking in rapid-fire bursts, holding her black bag over her head to block the rain and protect her hair knot. In a minute, she disappeared through the front door.

"So long, Bugs." Rand kept his eyes on his cellphone screen.

"See ya later, Alligator," Skylar gigged.

"After while, Crocodile."

"Thanks for taking us to the zoo," Skylar said. "It was fun. And don't worry about spilling ice cream on your shirt. Stuff like that happens to everybody."

I laughed. Skylar was a real sweetheart.

"Wow. This is crazy," Rand said.

"Let me see." Skylar leaned over to look at Rand's phone screen.

"What is it," I said.

"The storm," Rand suddenly sounded serious. "It's been upgraded to a major hurricane warning. Not just the usual stuff. The Doppler shows the storm out in the gulf and it looks huge. I mean mega-big. I've never seen one that big."

"That sounds bad," I said.

"Could be," Rand said. "Gotta go. Check you later, Bugs." He and Skylar hopped out of the back seat. Maria appeared in the doorway, motioning for the kids to hurry and get in out of the rain.

I watched Skylar race past her brother, who was waddling toward the house, still staring at his phone screen.

As the kids reached the front door, Susan's Range Rover shot out of the garage. I could see my daughter in the front seat, still yakking on the phone. She had donned her lucky, stylish blue and white bandana-scarf that not only protected the back of her neck from the sun, but also magically insured a sale. Or so she said.

Hurricane warnings. Hurricane watches. Hurricanes. Welcome to Florida.

I pulled back into the street and headed for home, my uneasiness ratcheting up into the danger zone.

CHAPTER 3

THE RAIN HIT THE TOWN Car in torrents as I passed the Emerald Fields Mall. My windshield wipers were in over their heads, so I took a left of Florida Avenue which was the most direct route to my beach house. The dashboard clock read 4:15 but the encroaching darkness forced me to turn on my headlights.

It was September and summer's halcyon days were drawing to an end. I turned on the car radio and listened to Paul Marriott's "Love is Blue." Lots of memories in that song.

I crept out of downtown, anxious to get home.

Bay St. Edwards sat on a peninsula that jutted out into the Gulf of Mexico with the bay on its north side. On the western end, where Susan and the children lived, the peninsula was connected to the mainland by the North Zephyr Causeway. The Causeway was an impressive feat of engineering but I always preferred good ole Highway 72, a two-lane road, located a few blocks from my beach house on the eastern end of the peninsula.

Bay St. Edwards was a cozy maritime community, but unfortunately, Susan and her developer buddies wanted to turn the place into a glitzy tourist trap by building cheap rental condos and beach houses with a sea view. For the time being, the peninsula was still a pleasant place to live. But it wasn't Colorado.

I saw a couple of kids in their late teens huddled under the overhang of a bus stop. A boy and a girl, their arms around each other, their shirts soaked, staring lovingly into each other's eyes, oblivious to the storm that raged around them.

For a minute, they looked like my old college teammate, Charlie Barnes and his girlfriend, later his wife, Barbie. After college, Charlie had gone to work for an insurance company in Fort Collins. Big Charlie had been a hell of a tackle in his day. Barbie became the executive director of a non-profit that helped homeless kids. She died of lung cancer a couple of years ago. Charlie hit the bottle. He died in a car wreck last year.

Suddenly the boy broke away from his embrace with the girl and trotted over to the Town Car. He even ran like Charlie, effortlessly but with purpose.

I rolled the window down half way.

"Hey Mister." The boy shot me a broad smile. "You got a second?"

"Sure. What can I do for you?"

The boy cleared his throat. "My girlfriend and I just got into town and to tell you the truth, we're a little short of cash."

I looked at the girl, who was still standing at the bus stop. She gave me a shy wave. I waved back.

"I was hopping maybe you could spare a couple of bucks."

The kid looked like a drowned rodent. But I had been young once and full of hopes and dreams and I suspected he was the same.

I fished out my wallet and pulled out a pair crumpled twenty-dollar bills.

The boy's eyes lit up.

I shoved the money through the window. "Welcome to Bay St. Edwards."

He took the money and his eyes were full of gratitude. "Thanks, Mister. You'll never know how much this means to us."

I nodded. "Stay dry," I said with a smile.

"Yessir. The boy snapped off a quick two fingered salute and trotted back to his girlfriend. Yeah. He ran just like Charlie.

Charlie was one the few teammates I kept up with over the years. After college, most us went our separate ways. They were a tough bunch and I missed them all. Of course, Tommy Liddell, our quarterback and my best friend, and I had stayed close. We'd made a formidable doubles team in handball, even won a few tournaments. We skied together for years and closed down a lot of bars in Vail and Winter Park.

A blast from a car horn behind me let me known the light had turned green.

CHAPTER 4

I WAVED AT THE KIDS, wiped a tear out of my eye and then drove on down Florida Avenue until I reached Highway 72 and turned left. Then I took another left at the dirt access road that led to my beach house, a block away from the beautiful Gulf of Mexico.

I pulled into the carport and listened to the last strains of "Born to be Wild" before turning off the radio. Born to be wild. Maybe once upon a time.

Inside the beach house, I went to the refrigerator and pulled out a bottle of Coors. A taste of home. My sofa faced the sliding glass doors at the back of the house and I sat down, put my feet on the coffee table, took a deep slug of beer and looked over the dunes at the waters of the Gulf.

The water was swirling and angry and the wind whipped debris all over the white sands. Whitecaps crashed on the beach. The daytime sky looked like midnight. I didn't bother to turn on the lights, preferring to watch the furious sea from the darkness of the beach house.

Sometimes nature was the best show in town, but the more I watched the Gulf, the more I realized I was scared as hell. I was witnessing Mother Nature pissed off big time.

I felt tired. I'd been on a long journey and my body was wearing out. Not that my body hadn't served me well. Years ago, I'd played fullback for the Northern State Wildcats. I'd served a tour of duty with the army in Vietnam. I'd hiked and skied the Rockies for years and played tournament level handball.

Since college, I'd maintained a daily routine of push-ups and sit-ups and free weights. I'd walked five miles on the beach every day after I'd moved to Florida. My hip hurt the whole way, but the pain went away after a couple of beers.

Lately, I didn't bother with any of it. Except the beer.

Susan was always telling me I should try bingo or shuffle board. But I couldn't see my 6'5" frame hunched over a shuffle-board stick. Truth be told, I was just killing time until it killed me.

I shuffled into the bathroom and opened the medicine cabinet, where rows of little brown plastic bottles greeted me. Too damned many of them. I grabbed one and popped a couple of Valium.

I wandered back into the kitchen and helped myself to another Coors. Back on the couch, I watched the pounding rain turn the sand into gray mud. The waters of the Gulf looked totally out of control, swirling and churning faster and faster.

This was how it ended. No more Megan, my wife of 30 years. No more mountains. No more handball. No more Charlie. No more classes to teach. Maybe it was time for the party to end.

It was something to think about.

MY BEACH HOUSE WAS A cramped wooden A-frame from the 1970s, solidly built, but showing a lot of wear and tear. Just like me.

I had furnished the place with odds and ends from a local consignment store—a black leather sofa, a rattan coffee table, a gray aluminum kitchen table with mix-matched chairs.

My TV didn't work most of the time. Sometimes I could have sound and no picture. Sometimes it was the other way around, but I didn't watch enough TV to make it worthwhile to get the set fixed.

I got another beer from the refrigerator, sat back down and looked out the sliding glass door. What had I gotten myself into?

Above the swirling whitecaps, the sky had turned a strange orange color like a fire behind smoke and the clouds had grown thicker and seemed so low they could touch the sea.

When you get older, the unfamiliar was always scary and the storm raging in the Gulf was the definition of unfamiliar. Something was bad wrong.

The technological revolution had left me far behind, but I opened the old laptop Susan had given me when she bought a new one and logged in.

I SCROLLED AROUND TO A couple of weather sites and found out there was a tropical storm centered in the Gulf, moving to the northeast. There were warning signals and alerts, but none of them sounded serious.

Outside, white shafts of lightening lit up the sky like ruptured spider webs. One of the sites mentioned a line storm—a severe squall that traveled in ominous dark lines across the water. They looked scary as hell, but Rand had assured me they were nothing to worry about. My gut told me otherwise.

Since I was already on the computer, I opened my email and clicked on a message that had come in a couple of days earlier. I'd read the note so many times I almost had it memorized. The subject line read "Sad News". The message that followed said: *Thought you'd want to know. He was a great guy. We had some times back in the day. You and me and Tommy and rest of the guys. If you get a chance, raise you glass to our good friend and our good times. Stay in touch. Matt.*

I clicked on a link at the bottom of the email and a picture of an old bald guy with spotted skin popped up. Underneath the picture the caption read:

Thomas Liddell, Local Banker, Succumbs to Cancer.

The article read: *Thomas Liddell of Denver. . . Rocky Mountain Bank, Vice President. . . Active in local charities. . . survived by his wife of 40 years and his two sons. . . Quarterbacked the Northern State Wildcats to a conference championship and a pair of wins in the Division II college football playoffs nearly a half century ago.*

The story didn't mention the nights me and Tommy and Matt and Charlie closed down the Satellite Bar and staggered home arm in arm. Or the conference championship game where we were five points down with seconds left. We drove to our opponent's goal line and Tommy knelt down in the huddle. He looked me square in the eye. "I'm calling your number big guy. Don't let me down."

And I didn't. Tommy called a power play up the middle to the fullback and I took the handoff and crashed into the end zone.

Only, in the end, I had let Tommy down.

I hadn't been there when he died. I didn't even make the funeral.

I lifted my beer bottle. "Good times and good friends," I said out loud in a choked voice.

I turned on the TV, hoping for some good news about the storm. The picture was fuzzy but the sound was okay. A weather guy in a crispy creased blue blazer stood in front of a map of the north Florida coast area. Red and green arrows showed wind flow. In the southern part of the Gulf, a swirling purple spiral pushed everything else aside. A flashing sign at the bottom of the screen read "Breaking News".

I cranked up the volume on the remote. The weather guy's voice sounded far away. Maybe Susan was right. Maybe I needed a hearing aid.

Outside, the rain lashed the glass door.

"And of course, this is the height of the hurricane season," the weather guy said. He was young and chirpy and his teeth looked like they would glow in the dark.

"Mid-August to late September. That's when we need to be on the lookout, folks. And this could be the first big one." He pointed to the ugly purple swirl and indicated that it could turn right and smash into Sarasota or turn left and head for New Orleans.

"At full force these babies can produce winds exceeding 155 miles per hour. A hurricane is a type of tropical cyclone that forms in the Gulf and they can bring heavy rainfall, floods, mudslides and high winds." His smile grew broader.

What the hell was the bastard smiling at? I looked out of the door and saw the angry water churn and crash on the beach. The sky grew darker. I was in a totally unfamiliar situation. All alone and growing more frightened by the minute. My uneasiness escalating exponentially. And the guy was smiling like he had just passed gas.

"Here's a quick reminder, folks," the weatherman said. "If the storm surge gets worse and it appears we might take a direct hit, disconnect cords from power outlets and unplug all electrical appliances. Watch out for the barometric pressure to fall. With what I'm seeing here, I'm afraid we're in for a long and dangerous night."

I had reached the stage of life where the universe took away more than it gave. There was not much to look forward to and it was often painful to look back. I'd never see Megan or Tommy Liddell again. I'd never play handball again. I'd never take my little girl down to the ice cream shop for a double chocolate cone. As if to remind me of where I was, I felt a shooting pain in my left hip. I straightened my leg and drained my beer.

Because I'd been so stupid, I'd never see the snow-capped Rockies again. Bay St. Edwards was the end of the line. My expiration date was drawing close. When I first got to Florida, Susan gave me some shit called Ginko Biloba, which was supposed to slow the aging process. Good luck with that.

My daughter was always giving me cheerful books on aging with chapter titles like "Don't be a Docile Fossil" or "Mind over Bladder." Truth be told, getting old was like being trapped in your own personal disaster movie. Every time you turned around, something was falling apart.

The Big Swim was the answer. I could wade into the Gulf and start swimming south until I saw Tommy and Charlie and all the other friends of mine who weren't here anymore.

I got another beer and drank it standing at the glass door, staring at the clouds and the crashing waves and thinking about the Big Swim.

Until somebody knocked on the front door.

CHAPTER 5

RONNIE CROW LOOKED DOWN AT the set of the weather broadcast and shook his head in disbelief.

"Don't worry, folks. There's nothing to be alarmed about." Ned Wallace, the local weatherman, beamed his broadest smile at the TV camera. "It's a typical tropical storm for this time of year. And we all know what that's like." He let out a little chuckle like he and his audience all shared a secret.

Up in the control room, Ronnie, who was a skinny intern, was getting a totally different view of the storm on his computer screen. He whirled around and looked at Barbara Stanhope, the program's executive producer. "Miss Stanhope. What's happening out there is a lot worse than a typical storm. Its. . ."

Barbara covered the mic on her headset with the palm of her hand.

"Ned's just so. . . hot," Barbara said. "He won't be around here long. The big markets will eat him up. Look at that smile and that hair. The man is a Greek god."

Ronnie looked away. Like all station employees, he knew all about the affair between the weatherman and his adoring producer.

It was late in the evening and the station was operating with a skeleton crew. Barbara was dressed casually in a lavender blouse and black slacks, her auburn hair tied back in a ponytail. "Go to the questions," she cooed into the mic.

Out on the set, Ned responded and Ronnie held his breath. "We've had lots of calls and tweets tonight about the storm," the weatherman said. "That's why we're bringing you this live weather update."

Ned's blue blazer was buttoned in the front and his jacket was augmented by a starched white shirt and a wine-colored tie. The creases on his gray pants were razor sharp.

"Start with the barometer," Barbara said to Bert, the technician in the control booth. Bert attacked his keyboard and the teleprompter leaped into action.

"A lot of you have asked about the sudden drop in the barometer we've seen lately," Ned said to the camera.

All things considered, Ronnie thought Ned was a total dumbass and didn't deserve Barbara. Ronnie thought Ronnie deserved Barbara. But he would never say anything. He was an intern.

"A sudden drop in the barometer signals the approach of high winds and bad weather," Ned said. "Like a giant vacuum cleaner, the low pressure in the eye of the storm is drawing the air south." He paused like he was waiting for applause.

"He's just so. . . hot." Barbara covered her mic.

"Winds blow in a counterclockwise spiral around the calm center, called the eye, which is anywhere between 20 and 30 miles wide." Ned squinted at the teleprompter for a second. "A category 2 can hit up to 110 miles per hour, a 3 up to 130 a 4 up to 155 and. . . "Ned paused for dramatic effect. "A category 5 hurricane hits at over

155 miles per hour. Now folks, let me reassure you, a category 5 hurricane is very, very rare."

Ronnie's eyes stayed glued to the computer screen, which was telling him a category 5 hurricane was not out of the question in the next few hours. Not as rare as you told them, Ronnie thought, looking at Ned in the studio.

"A lot of you have asked about how we name hurricanes," Ned said, moving on to another topic. "The first hurricane of the season starts with the letter A. Then B. Then C."

Ronnie hoped Ned wasn't going to cover the entire alphabet.

"Women's and men's names are now rotated. Up until 1979 only women's names were used for hurricanes. If that baby out in the Gulf turns into a full-fledged hurricane, we'll give it a man's name starting with the letter A.

Maybe they'll call it Hurricane Asshole, after you, Ronnie thought.

"And, of course, the names of especially severe hurricane's like Andrew and Camille and Katrina are retired," Ned said. "But please keep those questions coming in. We'll be with you the rest of the night. Our expert meteorologist will be monitoring the temperature, the pressure and the wind."

Expert meteorologist? He means I'll be monitoring the storm all night, Ronnie thought. I'll be tracking the hurricane while Ned and Barbara do the horizontal bop in the station manager's office.

"So, stay turned to WBEC and Eyewitness Weather right here in Crystal City. The eyes and ears of the Emerald Coast for news and weather. And now we'll send you back to our regular programing."

Ronnie tapped the keys of his computer. He was getting the same dire information everywhere. Something big was brewing.

CHAPTER 6

NED THREW OPEN THE DOOR to the control room. “Did I shine or what?” he said as he and Barbara exchanged high fives.

Ronnie rolled his eyes.

“God, what a job. All you’ve got to know is where the hot air is, where the cold air is, where it’s raining and where it’s not. I love it.” Ned did a couple of inexpert dance steps.

At least we’ll always know where the hot air is, Ronnie thought.

“Hey, Sport. How about getting me a cup of hot java from the break room?” Ned said to Ronnie.

Ronnie looked up. He suspected Ned always called him “Sport” because the weatherman had no idea what Ronnie’s name was.

“Sure, Ned. Be right back.” As Ronnie left the control room, he saw Ned slide his hand over Barbara’s scrumptious back side. “Lucky bastard,” the intern muttered as he headed for the break room.

Ronnie made his way down the hallway and checked out his reflection in the glass panel of the break room door. He didn’t like what he saw. His hair was stringy and needed washing, his effort to grow a beard was stalled out and his tattered jeans looked ridiculous in the station. He was in his last year as a meteorology major at Florida State and he knew his chance of ever hooking up with a woman as beautiful as Barbara Stanhope was the long shot of the century.

When he got back to the control room, he found Ned and Barbara huddled in the corner, speaking in low voices, inhaling each other's essence.

The intern handed Ned a coffee mug with "World's Greatest Weatherman" embossed on the side.

"Cream and double sugar, Sport?"

"Same as always," Ronnie said, heading for his computer.

As he sat down, he heard a loud slurp behind him. He hadn't spit in the coffee, but the thought had crossed his mind. He clicked on the Miami Weather site and started opening icons.

Across the room, Barbara began massaging Ned's shoulder.

"Holy shit!" Ronnie's head shot up from the computer screen.

Ned and Barbara jumped and Ned shot Ronnie a disapproving look.

"The storm," Ronnie said. "Out in the Gulf. It's picking up speed like crazy. Miami says it's already hit 75 miles per hour."

"Calm down, Sport," Ned said. "I don't think that's possible." He gave Barbara's backside a gentle pat.

"No. Look at this," Ronnie said.

Barbara pushed a stray lock of hair behind her ear. "Maybe we should take a look," she said to Ned.

Ned shrugged.

Ronnie realized his breath was coming in short gasps. In one lecture that he had never forgotten, this weird old eccentric professor at the FSU, a guy named Lauten Powell, who always wore cowboy boots and T-shirts to class, explained how a certain combination of sudden high pressure and low pressure could totally fool the Doppler. It would be an extremely rare occurrence, maybe once in a lifetime, but it could happen. Ronnie realized that was exactly the phenomena he was witnessing on the computer screen.

"When the storm surge hits, it's gonna be something." Ronnie said. "The storm should be losing intensity but it's not. Unbelievable. It's heading north and growing stronger."

Ned laughed. "Not to worry," he said. "This stuff happens all the time. Ever since Katrina, everybody gets their panties in a wad every time a squall kicks up in the Gulf. It'll slow down in a while. You mark my words."

Barbara broke away from Ned's caresses. "Humor the kid," she said, in her best executive producer voice. "What if he's right? Then we need to get you back on the air. We could be the first station to break the news."

Ned's lower lip protruded. "Look, Sugar Lumpkins," he said. "I know what I'm doing here. I checked the Doppler radar. It doesn't lie. It indicates the squall will change direction and die down."

"No. No. Look at this." Ronnie indicated his computer screen. "the high-pressure system will keep it from moving away. The low-pressure system will funnel the whole thing right at us. See. Miami says it's up to 90 miles an hour and gaining speed." If Professor Powell had been right, the storm was going to be a nightmare. The man always told his class to always be wary of relying too much on machines.

Barbara crossed the room, suddenly all business. "Show me."

Ronnie clicked another icon. A map of the region appeared on the screen, showing the swirling purple mass surging north.

"I told you," Ronnie said. "Look. The storm's heading for Destin and Santa Rosa Beach and Bay St. Edwards. We're only a few miles north. Holy shit! This is serious."

"Damn," Barbara said. "Ned. Get over here. I think the kid's on to something."

"If the storm keeps gaining speed," Ronnie said. "It's going to be a Cat 3 or 4 or maybe worse by the time it hits the panhandle."

"Let's just slow down here." Ned ambled across the room. "Try another site."

Ronnie punched in the website of the Tropical and Forecast Branch of the National Hurricane Center at Florida International University in Miami, which was a division of the U.S. National Weather Service.

It's already up to a Cat 2," Ronnie said.

"I'm going to call Jerry," Barbara said, referring to the station manager. Something's wrong here. With this kind of data, we should have heard from the National Oceanic and Atmosphere Administration people. Maybe some of their equipment has malfunctioned."

"No. Listen, you guys," Ronnie said. "I had this professor over at the U and he explained that. . ."

"Put a sock in it, Sport," Ned growled. "Let's see what Jerry says."

Barbara produced her cellphone and punched in the station manager's home phone number. She quickly pulled her device away from her ear and looked at the instrument like it was a dead rat. "All I get is a bunch of beeping noises. What the hell is going on?"

Ronnie pulled his own phone out of his pocket. "What's the number?"

Barbara told him and he punched in the station manager's phone number. "Same thing," he said.

"Oh, my god." Ronnie pointed at the computer screen. "Look at this. The storm is picking up speed. It's a hundred miles an hour now. The damn thing is moving way too fast."

Ned hooked his arm around Barbara's waist but she shook him off.

"We've got to get back on the air," the producer said. "We've got to warn the people down on the Emerald Coast."

"Maybe we should wait for Jerry," Ned said.

"Screw Jerry. Get back on the set."

Ned shrugged. "You're the boss." He headed for the door.

"Ronnie," Barbara said in a low voice. "What the hell is going on out there?"

The intern stared at the screen while he gnawed on the end of a pencil. "I'm not sure, Ms. Stanhope. But whatever it is, it's turning into a monster."

CHAPTER 7

"HOWDY, NEIGHBOR."

It was George Ferrell, the guy who lived in the next house down the beach. He was about my age, thickset with a shaved dome. George was friendly and outgoing like someone who drank too much coffee. I avoided him whenever I could.

"Come in. Get dry," I said in a feeble effort to sound neighborly.

"Don't mind if I do." George rushed past me, shedding his yellow slicker. "Hope I didn't catch you at a bad time."

"No problem."

George flopped down on the sofa.

"You want one of these?" I indicated the Coors in my hand.

"Don't mind if I do."

I retrieved a couple of beers, gave one to George and sat down in the chair opposite the sofa.

Outside, the rain pounded the house with machine gun intensity.

"Looks like I made it just in time," George said, waving his beer bottle at the rain. "I knew this baby was coming. It's gonna be a sonofabitch. I can tell you that."

I nodded.

"Say, are you okay? You look pale as a ghost."

"Friend of mine died back in Colorado," I said.

"Lot that going around with fellows our age." George shook his head. "Sometimes it seems like life is one big infantry patrol. We're all charging up a hill. Bullets raining down on us. We know one of those bullets will have our name on it before too long. Cancer, heart attack, stroke. But we keep slogging up the hill. It's tough to watch the bullets take out our friends one by one, but all we can do is keeping moving up the hill, hoping and praying the next slug ain't the one. Know what I mean?"

I managed a smile. George's metaphor wasn't too far off.

"Sorry for your loss." He took a generous pull from the beer bottle.

"Thanks."

"I reckon I better cut to the chase," George said. "This ain't a night to be hanging around, shootin' the shit. You know what I mean?"

I didn't consider talking about Tommy Liddell's death 'shootin' the shit', but I grunted my agreement.

"The missus told me I needed to talk to you. You ain't from around these parts and I'm willing to bet you ain't never seen what's about to happen."

"What are you talking about?"

"The hurricane that's brewing down in the Gulf. If it makes it this far, it's gonna be bad."

"TV weather guy says there's not much chance of that."

George shook his head. "Those TV fellows don't know their ass from crackers. I've lived in Bay St. Edwards all my life. Folks around here call me a Weatherbug."

I took a sip of my beer.

"See, here's the thing," George said. "You can read the intensity of a coming storm by watching the long swells and timing the duration between them as they hit the shore. I've been timing them all afternoon and I don't like what I see."

George was wound up and since I didn't know squat about Gulf storms, I let him ramble on.

"It's the rhythm of the waves," he said. "And this afternoon, I noticed they're rolling in way too fast. Faster than I've ever seen them. There's something out of the ordinary happening out in the Gulf. Something mean and ugly."

"Maybe the storm will swing away from us and hit the west coast of Florida or slam into New Orleans."

"That's what those TV chowder heads would tell you. Have you noticed that the last couple of days we've been having showers interrupted by sudden periods of calm?"

I hadn't paid any attention, but I nodded anyway.

"The last couple of weeks have been hot, humid and wet."

I assumed that was the way summer always was in Bay St. Edwards. Just like summer in hell.

"And we've had two coppery sunrises in succession. Any Weatherbug will tell you that ain't good." George leaned forward and locked me in an intense stare. "Late this afternoon, I watched the wild ducks. The flew around in a circle and then they just stopped. Little bastards were confused as hell."

So was I.

"You got another one of these?" George held up his beer bottle.

"Sure."

When I got back, George saluted me with his fresh beer. "The rats were the tipoff," he said.

"The rats?"

"Yeah. The rats. They told me there's one hell of a storm heading our way."

"The rats told you?"

"Right. I went down to the convenience store on Highway 72 late this afternoon. Got me a couple of bags of M&Ms. I can't get enough of those little suckers."

I began to suspect that George was coming unhinged.

"I saw the rats in the alley. Out behind the store. Hundreds of 'em. Big ones. Little ones. You name it. All of them heading in the same direction."

"Which was?"

George looked at me like I was the crazy one. "Inland. All the rats in Bay St. Edwards were fleeing inland. Getting away from whatever is out there in the Gulf."

"If that's true," I said slowly. "Then what do we do?"

"That's what I came to tell you. I'm hearing reports that the storm has already reached Warwick Harbor, just down the coast a ways. The main storm surge is going to hit Bay St. Edwards around dawn. You need to be ready to run like the devil was on your tail. Pack a bag—change of clothes, medicines, a flashlight, bottled water, a first aid kit. You won't have time to pack when the time comes."

Something sounded vaguely familiar about Warwick Harbor but I couldn't place it. I sensed an earnestness in George that made me uncomfortable. What if the old nut job was right? Talking to the rats? On the other hand, what did I care. Five minutes before he showed up at my door, I was about to take the Big Swim. What did I care if a hurricane hit?

"When the experts say evacuate, you run. You hear me? Don't waste a minute."

"Copy that."

George leaned forward and put his hand on my knee. He looked me straight in the eye. "John, the rats don't lie."

CHAPTER 8

THE STORM LASHED THE PLAYPEN Gentlemen's Club. The strip joint sat alone in a white-gone-to-gray single-story structure a few yards off Highway 72. Management had shut off the neon sign with the club's name and a silhouette of a nude woman in a provocative pose that hovered over the highway.

A gravel parking lot circled the building, but only three cars remained—a battered Ford pick-up, a mud-caked maroon Camry and a shiny jet-black Corvette. The cars were spaced out across the front of the lot like people in a bar who didn't want to talk to strangers.

Inside, dim lights concealed the worn carpet and nicked wooden bar stools. The Playpen reeked of lingering cigarette smoke, stale beer and body sweat.

"Why don't you shut it down, Harve?" Jackie Marsh flopped down on the bar stool next to the bouncer and manager for the evening. "I haven't had this much fun since I had root canal." The staccato pounding of the rain on the roof forced her to raise her voice.

"Boss said to keep her open till one." Harve Buckner was a muscular young man with stylish dark stubble on his face. He had been a high school wrestler and harbored ambitions of joining the police force until a burglary conviction dashed his dream. "But I hear you. By the way, thanks for coming in. We were pretty short-handed."

"Looks like," Jackie said. "Me and Rhonda." She indicated a skinny, pale girl who was half-heartedly waving her tiny breasts in the face of one of the club's two customers.

"That's the line-up," Harve said. "And Rhonda's clocking out after this set."

"Oh great. Just me and the pretty boys."

The two customers were identical twins, young men with fashionably cut whitish-blond hair. One of them had a dark streak in his hair above his ear.

"Polo shirts and Ralph Lauren slacks," Jackie said. "Not the usual greasy jeans and faded Metallica t-shirts. If I'm going to entertain those fancy boys, I need a scotch. On the house, Harve? For doing you a favor and working tonight?"

Harve smiled and nodded at the bartender. "On the house."

Wendy Chen, the bartender, fixed the drink and set the glass in front of Jackie. "Where you been keeping yourself, doll? We ain't seen you around much lately."

"I think I'm what they call semi-retired." Jackie took a sip of her drink. "Hell, we all know my days in this racket are numbered."

"Yeah, but I hear you were something up at the 4Play Club in Pensacola, back in the day," Harve said. "You're a legend up that way."

"That was long before your time, honey. But thanks for the compliment. Yeah, those were my glory days. I was the headliner. Every sailor in port wanted to check these out." She ran her hands over the t-shirt that covered her ample breasts.

Harve smiled. Even with her dark roots, smile wrinkles and a few extra pounds, Jackie Marsh was still a hell of a good-looking woman.

"But the Playpen is where all good strippers go to die." Jackie let out a throaty laugh and sipped her drink.

The wind attacked the building with renewed vigor, causing the windows to rattle. The rain on the roof sounded like a herd of mustangs galloping across the shingles.

From across the room, the twin with the dark streak in his hair signaled Wendy for another round of drinks. She acknowledged him with a nod and went to work behind the bar. "Chocolate martinis," she whispered. "Can you believe that?"

Jackie laughed.

"Takes all kinds," Harve said. "You better go change, Jackie. Rhonda keeps looking over here. I think she's about had it."

Jackie drained her drink. "I'm on my way," she said. "I'll send those fancy boys to heaven and back." She hopped off the bar stool and headed for the curtain beneath a sign that read "Employees Only."

"OKAY, FELLOWS. LET'S GIVE THE little lady a big hand," Harve said into the club's PA mic. He sat in a small booth overlooking the Playpen's two stages. The stage to his left was shrouded in darkness while dim lights rimmed the stage to his right. The stages weren't raised and featured a single pole in the center. The twins sat on padded chairs that ringed a waist-level wooden railing around the stage.

"And now on stage one, let's give it up for Vixen." The pounding of the rain on the roof drowned out his voice.

Jackie came out from behind a curtain in the rear of the club to the opening strains of a bouncy rap song. She was dressed in a sheer black jacket, a black G-string and a bra. She strutted onto the stage and spun around the pole but the twins barely looked up from their drinks and conversation with each other.

A set consisted of three songs. One with the jacket. One without the jacket and one without the bra and Jackie instantly knew that the next three songs were going to take forever.

The twin with the dark streak in his hair looked up at Jackie and playfully punched his brother on the arm. His brother looked up and leered.

Jackie danced over to them. She bent forward and gave them a good look at her own twins. "Evening, boys." Her husky voice barely carried over the pounding of the rain on the roof. "I'm Vixen. What's your name?"

She stuck out her hand and the twin with the dark streak shook hands with her. His grip was soft and clammy. "I'm Joel."

Jackie pulled her hand back. The man's eyes were wide and angry and didn't go with his coiffured hair and button-down appearance. "What's your pleasure, Joel? Besides those Chocolate martinis."

You name it, doll," Joel said. "Oxy. Vikes. Rushbos. Anything and everything that makes me happy. You want a little something?"

"No thanks." Jackie winked at Joel. "I'm strictly a white wine girl."

"This is my brother, Calder." Joel poked Calder in the ribs.

"We're twins." Calder let out a high-pitched laugh.

"Yeah. I kinda figured that." Jackie stepped back and swayed seductively to the beat of the music. She grabbed the pole, did a couple of spins, arched her back, stuck out her breasts and tried not to look bored.

At the beginning of the third song, Jackie went bare chested and danced over to the twins and shook her goods in their faces. Calder put a ten-dollar bill on the railing. If Jackie could get Joel to do the same, the evening wouldn't be a total bust.

Calder let out another cackle. "They ought to change the name of this shit hole," he said in a loud voice. "Call it the Pigpen."

"Or Fatties," Joel said. Both men cracked up with laughter.

"I'd call it 'Plumpers,'" Calder said and slapped the railing in time to his braying laughter.

"Okay, fellows. That's enough." Jackie stopped dancing and forced her face into a frozen smile. "My guess is if you two fuckweeds could do any better, you wouldn't be hanging around in a third-rate strip club like this."

"Oink, oink," Joel chanted. Calder punched him on the arm and joined the chant.

Jackie had seen the Corvette in the parking lot and figured the twins were a couple of rich guys slumming it for the evening. That usually meant big tips but this was garbage.

"Show's over, smartass." She grabbed her top off of the floor and covered her breasts. As she stormed past the twins, she snatched the ten spot off the railing.

Joel seized her wrist. "The show's not over until I say it's over." His eyes flashed intense anger. "I want you to wave those udders in my brother's face. That's what the ten bucks is for."

Jackie twisted her wrist, but Joel's python grip held firm.

Harve circled behind the stage, seized Joel's arm, twisted the limb behind him and shoved the arm upward. Joel let go of Jackie's wrist.

"What the hell? Stop it man. You're breaking my arm." Joel struggled to his feet and stretched upward on his toes to relieve the pressure.

Calder jumped out of his chair, his fists clinched.

"Don't even think about it," Harve said. "You make one move and I'll snap this asshole's arm like yesterday's kindling."

Joel moaned as Harve pushed the arm up again.

Calder froze.

"Like the lady said," Harve growled. "The show's over."

"Ahhh! Stop! Stop!" Joel squirmed as Harve shoved the arm further upward.

"It was a good show," Harve said. "Better than you clowns deserve. In fact, the show was so good, I know you want to leave Vixen a generous tip. Am I right or what?"

"Go . . ." Joel's retort was drowned out in an agonizing scream as Harve jammed the young man's arm toward his shoulder blade. "Okay, okay. Just ease off. Here." He fumbled in the pocket of his slacks and produced a wad of bills. Here. Take it bitch." A trio of twenties fluttered to the stage floor. God knows I can afford it."

A startled Jackie bent down and scooped up the money.

"Go home, Jackie," Harve said. "I'm closing the place down. The storm's getting worse. This is no night for anybody to be out. I'll escort these two gentlemen to their car and we'll all go our separate ways."

Jackie mouthed "thanks" at Harve and scampered out of the stage area and across the club to the little dressing room behind the "Employees Only" door.

When she came out, dressed in jeans and a blue hoodie, the twins were gone. So was Wendy, the bartender. Harve stood by the front door, smoking a cigarette.

"Sorry, Jackie," he said. "It takes all kinds. They went quietly. Pretty rich boys looking for kicks."

"I owe you," Jackie said.

"Just doing my job. You go home now. Get out of this weather." He opened the front door to the club, revealing sheets of wind and rain.

Jackie shuddered. "Good night, Harve. Thanks again." She lowered her head and raced across the parking lot to her Toyoda. By the time she piled into the driver's seat, she was soaked. She pulled back her hood, shook her hair and started the engine. It caught on the third try.

The Camry's tires crunched on the gravel as Jackie turned right on Highway 72, heading north for her apartment in Crystal City. The wind immediately shoved her car into the left lane. She wrestled the steering wheel back to the right.

The windshield wipers thumped furiously on the glass and Jackie had to wipe away the condensation on the windshield with the back of her hand. The beam of her headlights only extended a few feet into the dark, pounding rain. The dust up with the twins had rattled her and her breath came in sharp gasps.

CHAPTER 9

HARVE WASN'T SURE WHAT TO do.

Three deep cracks had appeared in the ceiling of the Playpen and they grew longer and wider in a matter of minutes. Water poured onto the floor. When the first crack appeared over the bar, Harve found a red plastic bucket in the utility room and placed it on the bar underneath the drip.

The second crack showed up a couple of minutes later over the stage where Jackie had gotten into it with the Blond Boys. Another bucket took care of the cascading water.

The Playpen felt depressing when it was empty and Harve thought the club felt claustrophobic. The odor of beer, cigarettes, cheap perfume and desperation seemed overwhelming.

The lights flickered.

"Shit," Harve said out loud. He circled behind the bar and turned on the tiny radio that sat under the bottle shelf. He twisted the dial back and forth until he heard a clear voice. *I cannot overstate the danger of the hurricane that is bearing down on the coast. This is not hype. This is the real thing.*

Harve felt the building shake and a cold chill ran down his spine.

The west side of Florida has never experienced a hurricane of this magnitude," the radio voice said. *The storm is barreling toward the Emerald Coast and should make landfall early in the morning. If you're in the storm's path...* Harve switched off the radio.

Just then the front door flew open.

Harve whirled around.

"We're back!" Two figures stood silhouetted against the driving rain. A flash of lightening reveled the blond twins in the doorway. They both wore long back raincoats and matching wide-brimmed black hats.

Calder let out a piercing laugh.

"We're closed," Have said. "Get outta here."

"Not yet, buddy-boy." Joel closed the door and the twins marched into the deserted club. Joel carried a baseball bat at his side and his brother, who was a step behind him, had a bicycle chain wrapped around the knuckles of one hand. The rest of the chain dangled at his side.

"Get outta here." Have's voice carried far more confidence than he felt.

Calder rattled the bicycle chain.

"We were just having some fun with that fat cunt and you ruined it," Joel said. "We didn't like that. And we don't like you."

Calder giggled again.

Harve bolted for the side door.

Joel raised the bat and rushed the bouncer.

Suddenly the whole building shook, causing a shelf of glasses behind the bar to come crashing down, shattering on the floor.

Calder laughed.

As Harve seized the doorknob, he felt a thump followed by a sharp pain in his shoulder. His arm and hand went numb. He lurched away from the blow and spun around.

Joel's teeth were set in an animal-like snarl, his eyes radiated evil as he raised the bat again.

Even though his arm was numb, Harve came in low and grabbed Joel around the mid-section. He hooked his leg behind Joel's calf and flipped him to the ground. When his assailant hit the floor, his breath whooshed out of him.

Harve slugged Joel in the face with a sharp left cross.

Then Harve's head exploded in pain.

The links of Calder's bicycle chain wrapped around his head, ripping off part of his ear. Harve's fingers automatically went to the spot where his ear had been. His hand came away drenched in sticky blood.

Calder looped the bicycle chain around Harve's neck. The bouncer felt the links bite into his skin as Calder jerked him away from Joel.

Harve struggled to his knees, but that was as far as he could get. Calder tightened the chain, and pulled, finding leverage by placing his knee in the center of Harve's back.

Joel rolled away from Harve and stumbled to his feet. His lip gushed blood from Harve's left cross. "Kill him! Kill him!" Blood spewed into the air.

Calder squeezed the chain and Harve tried to pry his fingers between the chain and his neck but the links were too tight. He couldn't breathe.

"Kill him! Kill him!"

Harve's hands were numb. Surely the twins would stop this insanity. You didn't kill anyone over a disagreement in a scuzzy strip club.

Rain gushed through the light fixtures, spreading cracks in the ceiling as water flooded the air conditioning vents. The building creaked and moaned.

Suddenly the world went black and the last thing Harve heard was Calder's maniacal laughter.

CHAPTER 10

AFTER GEORGE LEFT THE BEACH house, I sat down at the kitchen table. From that vantage point, I could keep one eye on the Gulf and one eye on the TV screen, which, at the moment, was filled with a *Law and Order* rerun.

I surfed around my laptop some more and found an electronic weather map that showed the swirling mass out in the Gulf. Like George predicted, a finger-like extension of the storm had already reached the coast, south of Bay St. Edwards. But George appeared to be the only person concerned about the gale.

My cellphone went off. My ringtone was a barking dog, which always startled me when I heard it. Rand had set it up and thought it was hysterical. I pushed the wrong button and a list of options filled the screen. I pushed another button. "Hello. Hello."

"Bugs? Oh, good. It's you." Skylar's voice was barely audible over the static. "Bugs. It's Skylar."

"I know, honey. Can you speak up? The connection's bad."

"It's the storm. Rand says storms can do that."

Outside, the wind slung a loose shutter against the side of the house. The rain swept across the back deck in thick sheets.

"Just speak up, Skylar and we'll be fine."

"Okay." Skylar raised her voice. "Bugs. Do you know where Mom is? She said she had a house to show down the coast, but that was a couple of hours ago."

"I don't know where she is, honey. But I'm sure she'll be back in a little while," I said.

"Maria's gone home and Rand and I want to go to the mall with the Roberts kids and see the new Spiderman movie. Ms. Roberts says the storm is nothing to worry about. She says you can't panic every time there's a storm in the Gulf and she's going to take us to the mall, but I don't want to go without telling Mom. Every time I call her, the phone just makes these weird beeping noises. I can't leave a message on her voicemail."

I wondered if I should tell Skylar to stay home. What if the stuff George told me was true? What if the storm surge hit the coast early? But what if George was a weather weirdo? The Roberts' mother didn't seem worried. Maybe these storms were routine in Florida. I took a deep breath.

"I'm sure your mom wouldn't mind," I said.

"Could you call her?" Skylar said.

"Sure. I'll give her a call and tell her where you guys are."

"Thanks, Bugs." Skylar sounded relieved. She said something else but either the connection or my fading hearing blocked it out.

I hit the wrong button again and a list of my contacts popped up on the screen. My eyes fell on the name "Liddell, Tommy." I needed to delete it, but I lacked the will. Deleting his name was like deleting Tommy. All traces of my best friend would be gone.

I punched Susan's number instead. Skylar was right. Nothing but beeping noises.

The wind blew a garbage can across my back deck. Damn. What had I done? Told the kids to go to the movies in the middle of a bad storm. Being a grandfather made me feel old. Like I should be sitting on the front porch whittling. Being a grandfather made me feel like the best part of my life was over. Some days Susan would ask me to babysit the kids and I'd turn her down. It would be the kind of day I wanted to stay home, be by myself, watch a ball game, drink a little beer, curl up with a good book. Be left alone. Susan called me an introvert only she made the word sound like 'serial killer'.

I sucked in another deep breath and stared out the glass door at the angry waters of the Gulf. Maybe it wouldn't hurt to pack a bag like George said. I could always unpack it in the morning.

I drifted back into the bedroom, where I pulled down my weathered backpack from the top of the closet. The pack was like an old friend. For twenty years, the knapsack had carried my gear on hiking and snowshoeing trips back in Colorado and there was something comforting in just holding it in my hand.

I tossed the backpack on the bed, opened the flap and stuffed in a clean shirt and a pair of slacks, some boxer shorts, a collection of little brown pill bottles, a giant bottle of ibuprofen, a flashlight, my old Swiss Army knife and three bottles of water. Back in the kitchen, I found a variety pack of power bars and crammed all of them into the backpack.

I dropped the backpack by the front door. Just in case the rats were right.

Back in the kitchen, I tried Susan's number again. Beeps and boops.

I sipped another beer and watched the tail end of an old Steve McQueen movie on TV. A strip along the bottom of the screen let me know the hurricane warning remained in effect.

Fatigue, beer and Valium crept over me. I lay down on the sofa and folded my hands behind my head. I felt a lifetime of tired and realized I was too exhausted for the Big Swim. Maybe another day.

Off in the distance, I could hear the wind lashing the side of the house and the waves crashing beyond the dunes. Where was the snow? The mountains? Where was home?

I tumbled into a deep, troubled sleep.

CHAPTER 11

BARBARA STANHOPE PACED THE CONTROL room of the TV station, clutching her clipboard to her chest. The only sound in the room was the click-click-click of Ronnie Crow's computer keys.

"Looks like we're in for a long night," Barbara said. Her voice radiated her nervousness.

"Yes, ma'am."

"You like this weather stuff, don't you?" Barbara said.

Ronnie looked up from the keyboard. "I love it," he said. "Ever since I was a kid. Studying meteorology has been the highlight of my life." A hint of a smile crept across his face. "I don't do much else. I suck at sports and video games."

"Tell me what's coming," Barbara said. "I've never been in a hurricane." The producer felt fear crawling down her spine. She couldn't trust Ned. Nothing bad ever happened in Ned's world. He looked good in front of the camera. He chased women. That was his universe. But Ronnie Crow knew the score.

"For one thing," Ronnie said. "Few events on earth can rival the power of a hurricane. What's so scary about this one is it's so unpredictable. I can't tell what it's going to do. But the way it's picking up speed is frightening. It's already hit the Emerald Coast, but look at this." He indicated his computer screen. "There's still a part of it swirling around in the Gulf and, as far as I can tell, it's getting bigger and picking up speed. And that's really scary."

"That bad, huh?"

"Yeah. That bad. Some experts think the dinosaurs were wiped out by a series of prehistoric hurricanes. Storms like that can churn the sea in fifty-foot peaks. The winds can take out buildings."

"You think this new storm could be like that?"

"Could be."

Out in the studio, Ned appeared on the set. He hooked up his mic and straightened his tie.

Barbara flipped down her own mic from her headset.

"Ms. Stanhope," Ronnie said, furiously tapping keys on his keyboard. "The storm is building a lot of energy as it races across the Gulf. It's sucking up warm air from the surface and then dispensing cooler air into the atmosphere. It's. . . it's breathing in and out. Like a giant dragon."

Barbara stared at him.

Ronnie nodded. There was nothing left to say.

"We'll get you back to your regular programming in a minute, folks." Ned faced the camera, flashing his toothy, reassuring grin. "But first we've got an important weather update from the National Weather Center."

Behind him, multi-colored graphics showed rain and wind pounding the coast from Tampa Bay to Mobile, Alabama. But the main attraction remained the swirling purple mass in the Gulf. The monster was heading north.

"It's now official, folks. We're looking at the first real hurricane of the season," Ned said. "The National Weather Center has designated the storm Hurricane Atlas. That's a heck of a name if you ask me."

Barbara shook off the shock of what Ronnie had told her. "Precautions," she said into her mic.

"Atlas has picked up enough speed to be considered a Category 3 storm. That means it might be time to take a few precautions, people. You might want to nail a few boards on your windows and check those flashlight batteries." Ned grinned and chuckled.

Ronnie shook his head in disbelief.

"Ned!" Barbara barked into her mic. "Wipe that stupid grin off your face. You're talking about people losing their homes."

A momentary shadow passed over the weatherman's face but he recovered quickly, producing a frown suitable for a funeral. "I know a lot of you have seen the lightening this evening. Pretty awesome, huh? Looks like fireworks against the back sky. But don't be alarmed. That's a natural phenomenon. Ole Mother Nature just feeling her oats."

Barbara gritted her teeth. "Tell them what to do."

Ned smiled into the camera. "Okay, people. Here's a short list of some practical things you can do to be ready if Atlas hits the Emerald Coast. . ."

"Ms. Stanhope," Ronnie said from behind his computer screen.

"Yeah, kid."

"The National Weather Service just updated Atlas to a Cat4. The storm is picking up speed like crazy."

"Any sign it's turning?"

"None. It's heading straight for the Emerald Coast."

"What was Katrina?"

"A Cat5."

"You don't think---"

"There's no way of knowing."

"Damn."

Ronnie swiveled around in his chair so he could face Barbara. "There's another problem if the storm hits the coast."

"And what's that?"

"Down the coast," Ronnie said. "Around Bay St. Edwards. They've been doing a lot of building down there. The developers have started putting in shopping malls and condos and stuff."

"What about it?"

"Well, the problem is they've built over a lot of coastal marshlands that provided a buffer from flooding and storm surges. If a Cat3 or higher hurricane hits that area those people are going have major flooding problems."

"Shit," Barbara said.

Ronnie swiveled back around to his computer, where his fingers flew over the keys. "Oh, God," he said. "Look at this."

Barbara crossed the room and looked at the screen. "Ned! Ned! This is important. Listen. Say this just like I tell you. No jokes, no ad libs. Do you understand?"

Back in the studio, Ned was wrapping up the weather alert. "So stay tuned to Eyewitness News. We'll be here all though the night with bulletins and weather updates. And just remember. . . oh, I've just gotten some important breaking news. The National Guard has been put on alert. All police departments and fire departments all along the Emerald Coast have been put on alert. All hospital personnel need to report to their jobs immediately." Ned managed a last smile.

Up in the control booth, Ronnie and Barbara exchanged terrified looks.

CHAPTER 12

TEN MINUTES AFTER SHE DROVE away from the Playpen, Jackie Marsh knew she had made a mistake. The Camry's windshield wipers couldn't handle the torrential rain and the wind made the car drift and sway on the slick highway. She slowed to a crawl. Even then, she couldn't see the shoulder of the road and the yellow line in the center of Highway 72. She was flying on instruments.

Jackie crept north toward Crystal City, but at the rate she was traveling, it would daybreak before she got to her apartment.

What a night. First the Stupid Twins and now the worst storm she's ever seen. Look in the dictionary under "creepy" and you'd find the blond twins. Jackie had seen her share of leering, zonked out idiots in her day. But those two. There was something seriously off about them. Something that was more than too much booze or too many pills. There was serious meanness. Serious evil.

Thinking about the twins made Jackie shiver.

How had it come to this? Wacked out twins in the Playpen making fun of her. Laughing at her body. Humiliating her.

But her world had never been a safe place. As if to prove her point, the wind shoved her Camry into the shoulder of the highway. Jackie jerked the steering wheel back to the left with both hands and steadied the car, then she slowed down even more. The rain pounded the roof of the car.

Twenty years ago, Jackie Marsh had been a high school student in Toledo, Ohio, the only child of a violent, alcoholic mother who beat her with a belt and burned her with cigarettes. Her father had bailed out when she was in diapers. Despite her mother, Jackie had become a good student and harbored dreams of going to college.

She had clerked at a mom and pop store and had saved enough money to go on her high school's senior trip to the Emerald Coast of Florida, a fun romp all of her classmates eagerly anticipated.

But Jackie's mother had found her money in a cigar box under her bed and binged at the local liquor store. When Jackie got home, her mother took the belt to her for complaining about the missing money.

A few days later, Jackie borrowed small amounts of cash from every friend she had, including a sympathetic math teacher, and joined her classmates on the road to the Emerald Coast.

The coast was like heaven to the Toledo kids. They swam in the Gulf, parasailed, ate fresh seafood, went deep sea fishing and built a fire on the beach and ate smores. Romances blossomed.

After five wonderful days, the class returned to reality and Toledo. All of the class except Jackie Marsh. Jackie slipped a note under the door of the chaperones' motel room, explaining that she was over eighteen and chose not to return to Ohio.

A frantic search followed, first by the chaperones and Jackie's classmates, then by the local police. But Jackie Marsh was gone. The authorities eventually concluded that because of her age, she was within her rights.

Jackie Marsh was on her own in paradise.

A STOP SIGN BLEW ACROSS the highway, barely missing Jackie's Camry and causing her to suck in a frightened breath. She was five miles from Crystal City, but it seemed like forever. She drummed a nervous rhythm on the steering wheel as the car inched along.

The radio yielded nothing but static. She tried Art's number on her cellphone. Art was the latest in a long line of boyfriends. He was a truck mechanic who had been between jobs for over a year while he lived in Jackie's apartment. He had dark hair, dark eyes and amazing tats. That almost made up for the fact that he was a total dimwit.

The cellphone was dead.

Up ahead, Jackie saw the flashing blue light of a police car, parked on the side of the highway. A state trooper in a yellow slicker stood in the middle of the road, signaling for Jackie to stop.

The trooper approached the driver's side of the Camry. "I'm sorry, ma'am, but Highway 72 is closed from here to Crystal City. Trees are down, low places are flooded." He had a gentle Southern drawl. "We can't keep barricades up because the wind keeps blowing them away," he shouted over the howl of the wind.

"But I live in Crystal City," Jackie stammered.

The trooper shook his head. "Doesn't matter. You couldn't get through even if you tried. You gotta turn around. Find someplace to get out of this storm."

Jackie nodded. There was no point in arguing.

"Find shelter as soon as you can," the trooper said. "Maybe you could head back down 72 and cut through to Bay St. Edwards. Go across the causeway and get to Crystal City that way. That might be your best bet."

"I guess I don't have any choice."

"No, ma'am. I don't think you do. We're in for a big one. The power is out all over the region. Headquarters can't get any info. Nobody knows what to expect."

Jackie swallowed. "I hear you," she said. "Thanks for the warning. I'm on my way. You take care now."

"You too." The trooper gave her a friendly salute and trotted back to the shelter of the police car.

Jackie made a U-turn and headed back down the highway. The rain pounded the Camry with relentless fury and spider web lightening filled the sky as the car crawled down the road.

After a while, Jackie was aware of an odd sensation. It was a combination of feeling totally alone combined with unrelenting fear.

CHAPTER 13

"MIT DID A STUDY IN 2005," Ronnie Crow said, never taking his eyes off his computer screen. "Their atmospheric scientists found that hurricanes have grown significantly more powerful and destructive over the last three decades."

"So this thing we're watching may not be that unusual?" Barbara looked over Ronnie's shoulder at his computer terminal. The sudden rush of Barbara's perfume left the intern disoriented for a moment. "Hurricanes. . ."

"We can't put that on the air." Ned cut Ronnie off in mid-sentence. "Our audience thinks global warming is a crock of liberal do-gooder manure. They won't believe anything I say if I start blaming the hurricane on global warming."

Barbara flashed Ned an irritated look. "I doubt they care at this point," she said. "They want to know if their homes and their lives are in danger. They don't give a rat's ass why. Political correctness doesn't matter at that point."

"I still don't think I should mention global warning on the air," Ned said like a scolded schoolboy.

“Fine,” Barbara snapped back. “But you’ve got to go on the air in ten minutes and tell our audience we missed the boat earlier. You’ve got to warn them that a hell of a storm is heading our way.”

Ronnie clicked more keys. “This is incredible,” he said. “According to the latest NHC data, the winds in the Gulf have already hit 120 miles per hour. How can that be?”

“Oh, god.” Barbara’s hand went to her mouth. “My father is in a Crystal City nursing home. Surely they have some kind of hurricane protocol at the home.”

“I’m sure they do,” Ronnie said. “I think there are all kind of regulations that cover that. I’m sure your dad will be okay.”

Barbara patted Ronnie’s shoulder. “Thanks.”

“From what I’m looking at here,” Ronnie said. “Somehow, out in the Gulf, the air near the surface has become superheated. Man, that’s scary. This thing is weird. You can throw out the rule book on this one.”

“I can’t go on the air and say that,” Ned said. “Why don’t I say something like ‘we can expect winds up to 50 or 60 miles an hour but the winds will probably start dropping by the time the storm reaches shore?’”

“That’s what they said in ’92,” Barbara said. My aunt down in Dade County told me all about it. She said the weather forecasters underplayed what was about to happen. It turned out to be the worst natural disaster in U.S. history. The winds rose to over 150 miles per hour.”

“Oh, come on, Barbara” Ned said. “We’re not looking at anything like that here.”

“We could be,” Ronnie said, looking at Ned. He could tell the weatherman wanted to smack him in the chops.

“Galveston in 1900 was a CAT-4,” Ronnie looked back at the screen “Killed 8,000 people.” Winds over 140 miles per hour. We could easily be looking at something like that here.”

Ned filled his cheeks and exhaled. “Okay, Sport. That’s enough. Crawl back into your computer and keep your mouth shut. Let the grown-ups handle this.”

Ronnie looked up and frowned at Ned.

“Stop it, you two,” Barbara said. “We’ve got work to do. We’re back on the air in six minutes. Ned. Go do whatever you do to look like at movie star. Ronnie. Get me the latest dope from the Hurricane Specialist Unit. Come on, guys. Let’s get going.”

CHAPTER 14

WE INTERRUPT THIS PROGRAM TO *bring you an emergency alert. I repeat. This is an emergency alert.*

I woke up to the sound of a panic-stricken voice. I had left TV on all night.

I repeat this is an emergency alert!

I had spent the night on the sofa. Too many beers and pills. Waking up took a major effort. I didn't have a clue what time it was. The light, what little of it there was, was an odd yellowish gray. The wind howled and the rain pounded the roof of the beach house. I'd slept in my khaki slacks and maroon golf shirt, which added to my state of confusion.

Letters scrolled across the bottom of the TV screen. *The outer winds of Hurricane Atlas have hit the Florida Coast. The affected areas include Rosewater Beach, Bay St. Edwards and New Britten Township. The storm surge has started and residents in those areas are advised to stay in their homes. This is an official emergency alert.*

I tossed my blanket on the floor and swung my legs over the side of the sofa. Sharp pains radiated across my lower back, down my hip to my knee.

All residents should take immediate cover.

I took a couple of halting steps and the pain receded. At least a little.

The wind sounded like a jet engine. Outside the sliding glass door, rain pounded the deck. The palm trees by the dunes weren't swaying any longer because the wind had bent them over double. What looked like roof tiles were blowing everywhere. I could hear a steady thudding caused by deep ocean swells falling on the beach. That was what George the Weatherbug had been talking about. The sound was nature's warning that it was time to save your ass.

My hands trembled with fear. I was in the middle of a nightmare and couldn't wake up. I limped into the master bathroom, where huge cracks that looked like spider webs decorated the ceiling. I tossed four ibuprofen tablets into my mouth and turned on the water. Nothing came out.

Holding the pills in my mouth, I hobbled back into the living room, grabbed the last bottle of beer from the night before off the coffee table and washed down the medicine.

The house creaked and moaned like it was in agony. Suddenly the Monet print in the hallway plunged straight down and shattered on the hardwood floor. "Shit." I sucked in a frightened breath.

The TV came off the wall and crashed to the floor. Glass flew everywhere. I looked out the windows and saw roof tiles swirling around like they had been fired out of a thousand canons.

My heart pounded like crazy and I wondered if I was going to have a heart attack, which is always a looming possibility at my age.

I forced myself to focus. Coming unglued wasn't going to help anything. Despite the TV warning to stay home, my house was not going to withstand the assault much longer. Fight or flight went down the drain. Flight was the only option.

I limped back into the bedroom, where the dry walls bubbled up on all sides. In the closet, I rummaged through the pockets of the only suit I had left from Colorado. In the inside jacket pocket, I found a wad of neatly folded bills, held together with a rubber band. Three hundred bucks. Even in the apocalypse a few dollars seemed like a good idea.

As I headed back into the living room, the wall phone in the kitchen started ringing but the sound was barely audible over the screaming of the wind.

I picked up the receiver.

Attention! Attention! The incoming hurricane is now officially a Category 4 and increasing in velocity. A mandatory evacuation has been declared for the following counties: Sebastian, Greene, Garland, Bay St. Edwards and Washington.

A robo call. I was listening to a machine. One machine said stay in my house. Another machine told me to run like hell. I had a strong suspicion that nobody knew what to do. The thought was not comforting.

The robotic voice kept going but the howling wind plus my hearing loss made listening tough. I heard something that sounded like "Cat5." The machine couldn't mean "Category Five" as in a Category 5 hurricane. That was impossible. Rand told me those things only happened once every century or every millennium.

We were a culture that relied on technology. We couldn't scratch our collective ass without checking with the smartphone or Googling or going on social media. But technology had failed. Stay in your home. Evacuate. The machines had missed a Category 5 hurricane. I guess ultimately people ran the machines and people made mistakes.

I looked out the window in time to see more roof tiles, more debris and a couple of canvas chairs sail past my deck. The sky had turned a furious reddish-yellow color. The glass in the door cracked.

A house down the beach blew apart like it was made of Legos, sending the walls sailing in different directions. The roof hurdled across the sky followed by sticks of furniture.

For a moment I was literally paralyzed with fear. I couldn't move. The whole world was coming apart. My circuits were overloaded and the terror inside me was like a burning fire that was frying all my nerve endings. The world was rapidly coming to an end.

Then I thought about Susan and the kids. What was happening to them? I scooped up the cellphone from the coffee table and punched in Susan's number. The damn thing had gone silent. I went to the texting thing and typed in "R U Ok?" and punched the "Send" button. A message appeared that my note could not be sent. My anxiety rocketed to the next level.

I stuffed the phone in my pocket.

In the distance, out where the dunes used to be, I saw George's house bobbing out to sea on the surging waves. I couldn't look away. George's prediction had come true. The rats were right. George had read the signs and gotten the hell out of Dodge while the gettin' was good.

When the canned goods blew off the pantry shelf and sailed across the room like missiles, I snapped out of my zombie state and decided to abandon ship. Fast.

I limped to the front door and slipped into my sturdy Colorado hiking boots. Tough footwear with thick treads. Susan had hooted at me for bringing them to Florida, but Susan hooted at me for a lot of things. I grabbed my backpack.

The front door opened inward but the winds had created a vacuum and, no matter how hard I pulled, the thing wouldn't open, so I set down the backpack and gripped the handle with both hands. Pain from my arthritic knuckles shot up my arm. I ignored the pain and gave the door one final heave-ho and it swung open, letting in a powerful gust of wind.

I snatched my backpack off the floor and slipped through the opening. A half dozen steps away from the house, the wind blew me off balance and I went down to one knee just as the furniture blew out of the door behind me. I threw myself flat on the ground until the rain of chairs and tables stopped.

When I stood up, the force of the gale hurled me against the side of the beach house. Panic washed over me. This was worse than anything I'd encountered in Vietnam. This was the whole universe out of control. This was the whole world ending.

Clutching my backpack to my chest, I inched around the beach house, planning to make a break for the highway. When I reached the side, I stole a glance back at the Gulf. Like a wild animal suddenly released from a cage, a mountain of blue-green water at least thirty feet high was rolling over the remaining dunes and heading straight for me.

CHAPTER 15

JACKIE MARSH WOKE UP WITH her face mashed against the passenger side window of her Camry. Dried blood covered the front of her hoodie and when she put her fingers to her cheek, they came away red.

She pushed herself upright and looked out of the spider webbed crack in the front windshield. Chairs and shutters and tree branches bobbed aimlessly in the shallow waters of the lagoon. A few feet away, a Honda Accord was wrapped around a palm tree.

Off to the left, Jackie saw the shell of a weather beaten building she recognized as the Smiling Fish. Great clam chowder. Super fish sandwiches. Now the sidewall was gone and a speedboat had been rammed through the front of the restaurant. Half of a highway billboard lay upside down on the Smiling Fish's oyster shell paving.

Jackie's lower lip trembled. She sucked in a series of deep breaths as the night before flooded back into her mind. She had looked the Grim Reaper square in the eye and slapped the old bastard silly.

After the state trooper had turned her around on Highway 72, she had driven south in an effort to get through Bay St. Edwards and make it to the Zephyr Bay Causeway, which would have taken her back to her apartment in Crystal City.

Only she never made it.

The wind and rain had picked up in intensity with each mile she drove and leaves, solid white with salt spray, had rained down on her car like giant snowflakes.

By the time she turned right on Florida Avenue, she knew she wasn't going to make the causeway. The wind had pushed her car onto the shoulder like the Camry was a toy.

Cars and boats sailed past her, carried on the wind. She frantically looked for some kind of shelter. Getting out of the car would be suicide even though Bay St. Edwards was less than a mile away.

In desperation, she pulled onto a side road that was lined with shops and restaurants. Maybe one of the buildings might offer cover. Anything to get out of the raging squall.

Through the overwhelmed windshield wipers, Jackie saw the Smiling Fish on her right. The Fish sat nestled next to a small inland lagoon that was surrounded by trees. If she could get inside the building, maybe the Fish had a basement or a bathroom with no windows where she could wait out the storm.

She stomped the accelerator.

The gale force wind and mountainous waves slammed into the Camry and lifted the car off the ground, shoving it toward the Smiling Fish, spinning it around and around.

Jackie screamed and gripped the steering wheel until her fingers ached from the effort. She knew she was screaming but couldn't hear her own voice, which was drowned out by the yowling wind.

The car titled on its side and flew forward. Jackie held on to the steering wheel like a child on a fast roller coaster. Then the car flipped upside down.

Hours later, Jackie was still alive.

The storm had thrown her sideways, snapped her seatbelt and banged her head against the passenger side window. She dug a Kleenex out of her purse and wiped the blood off her cheek and forehead. Her insides refused to stop trembling. There was a knot the size of a baseball on her temple and her head ached like the hangover from hell.

But she was alive.

The car door jammed, but Jackie forced it open with her shoulder. Her first couple of steps were little more than a drunken stagger, but she quickly regained her balance as the blood returned to her legs. The front of the Camry was crushed.

A light rain peppered the Smiling Fish parking lot and Jackie felt chilled so she dug a spangled blue jean jacket out of the back seat of her car and tossed her blood-stained hoodie into a ditch.

She looked around for signs of life but didn't see anybody. Nothing but a wasteland of downed trees and smashed cars.

She cautiously made her way toward the Smiling Fish, wading through smelly, ankle-deep water, praying she wouldn't step on a broken bottle.

Jackie climbed around the boat that had crashed through the front door of the Fish and went into the restaurant. The place was trashed. Tables and chairs overturned and tossed against the walls, bottles from the bar smashed. A ceiling fan had collapsed and lay shattered on the floor.

"Hello. Hello. Is there anybody here?"

Nothing but an eerie silence.

Back outside, she felt hungry and her mouth was parched. She assessed her options, which felt pretty limited.

She figured her best bet would be to hike back to Florida Avenue and hitch a ride into Bay St. Edwards. Fortunately, she was wearing a pair of running shoes and walking would be easy.

Only, a hundred yards down the road, she discovered that the ground was covered with a couple of inches of water and within minutes, her feet were soaking wet. Dark, threatening clouds dipped and swirled like they were being whipped with a giant mix master.

But she wasn't going to give up. Not now. Not ever. That was what her mother had done. She had given up on life. She had just quit. No more hopes and dreams. Just booze. She let her appearance slide and spent her days in front of the TV set, soaking up the bourbon.

Jackie knew she had overcompensated out of her fear of winding up like her mother. Jackie was upbeat and positive. She kept her hopes and dreams alive. College. A nice guy. She was determined to be more than a washed-up stripper. She had more to offer the world than a pretty set of boobs.

But she knew her positive attitude often crossed the line into what she once read was called "toxic positivity." In trying to be positive, she ignored reality. She suspected that surviving a hurricane might change that.

Sloshing through the drizzling rain to Bay St. Edwards, she hiked up the collar of her blue jean jacket and concentrated on putting one foot in front of the other. Nothing else mattered. Bay St. Edwards wasn't that far, maybe an hour.

Jackie put one foot in front of the other and propelled herself forward because, if nothing else, Jackie Marsh was a survivor. In an earlier age, they would have called her a tough broad. She had survived every blow life had dealt her. A hurricane and a car wreck?

Bring it.

CHAPTER 16

I DIDN'T HAVE TIME TO think. As the giant wave attacked the dunes, I fled across the highway in a limping, scrambling shuffle, hightailing it across the road to a small strip mall. A dog grooming parlor, a lawyer's office, a dance studio, a liquor store, a financial advisor's office.

When I reached the strip mall, the windows were blown out of all the storefronts and the air held the odd perfume of booze from all the shattered bottles in the liquor store.

The financial advisor's office was on the corner, so I climbed through the broken glass of the store front, yelled a perfunctory "hello" a couple of times but nobody answered. I could hear the roar of the giant wave getting closer and closer so I sought refuge beneath the spiral stairwell that led to the upstairs.

I curled into a ball and shielded my head with my backpack as the wind slammed debris against the front of the building. I looked up and saw street signs, a bicycle and a park bench. An SUV slammed into the reception area of the office with an ear-splitting crash.

The jet engine howl of the wind intensified and rain assaulted the building. When the giant wave hit, it rocked the foundation of the strip mall. The wall shook and water cascaded through the front door and windows. The water was filthy and stank of decay.

I cringed underneath the backpack and prayed the roof wouldn't collapse on my head. My heart raced to the point I was sure I was going to have a heart attack. No heart could stand that much adrenalin.

Maybe it was just as well. I suspected I'd stayed too long at the party. As Don Meredith used to say, "turn out the lights, the party's over." Death was everywhere. In the screeching of the storm, the smell of decay, the flooding water, the quaking of the building. I was about to die. This was how it ended. Drink it in, John. These are your last moments on the planet.

Only it didn't end.

The wind finally subsided. The water receded. Objects stopped slamming into the strip mall and the world grew still.

After a while, I crawled out from under the stairwell. My hip throbbed and my breath came in short gasps. I trembled like I was standing on an iceberg as I waded across the lobby of the office. The water was knee high and papers and folders bobbled in the salty flood.

I eased past the SUV and crawled out of what remained of the office door. When I looked up, I found myself on what might as well have been another planet. The end of the strip mall was gone. Off to my right, where houses had been, there was a field of concrete slabs.

Uprooted trees lay scattered across what I thought was the highway, although it was covered in several inches of water and it was impossible to tell where the road was really located.

The trees that hadn't been uprooted were covered with salt, which gave them an eerie appearance like ghosts serving sentry duty.

I did a quick inventory of my own well-being. A few cuts and scrapes. A bump on my head.

My beach house should have been across the highway and down the sands toward the Gulf, but there was nothing there.

I didn't have a clue what to do next. I knew there had to be some kind of protocol, but if there was, only Floridians knew what it was. I was a Colorado guy. A Colorado guy trapped in a surrealistic nightmare.

As soon as the shock subsided, my anxiety about Susan and the kids came roaring back. How bad had the Emerald Fields Mall been hit? My phone was relatively dry so I tried Susan's number again. Beeps and boops. Not even a robo message.

Out came the little keyboard. "R u ok?" I was convinced that texting was corrupting the language, but it hardly seemed like the time to stand on principle.

I sent the same message to Skylar's number and sat down on a block of concrete that had been ripped from the strip mall and waited for an answer. Several minutes passed. Nothing. I gave up and stuffed the phone back into my pocket.

A few feet from where I was sitting, clogged storm drains vomited their excess back onto the already flooded streets. Leaves and junk floated and bobbed in the water. Then the things in the water started moving on their own, small black knots popping up and moving toward me.

Snakes.

Good sized snakes. Thick and black and mean looking. I'd heard about cotton- mouth water moccasins when I'd first moved to Bay St. Edwards but on sight I didn't know the difference in a water moccasin and a water buffalo. Okay, I did know that, but a cottonmouth and a garden snake could have been twin brothers as far as I was concerned.

All I knew was I wanted to get as far away from the snakes as fast as I could.

As I sloshed away from the snakes, seeking higher ground, I saw a figure shuffling toward what remained of the strip mall from further down the highway.

CHAPTER 17

THE FIGURE WAS AN OLDER woman, dressed in jeans and a gray T-shirt. She was soaking wet. She wasn't walking so much as she was doing an odd zombie shuffle. I walked toward her and we met next to the rubble that had once been the liquor store.

"Hello," I said.

The woman nodded. Her eyes were glassy and a streak of blood had dried on her face from a nasty gash on her forehead. Her skin was waxy and pale. She stopped and looked right through me.

"Are you alright?"

"Armageddon has come," she said.

"It sure felt like it."

The woman's body swayed as if she was listening to some far away music only she could hear. "My house is gone." Her voice was flat and emotionless.

"Mine too."

"My new dining room table. I just got it. Saved up the money for it. The table was so pretty. It's gone too."

"I'm sorry."

"Everything blew up. A gas leak. Bob flicked his cigarette lighter and everything blew up. I told him to quit smoking. Old fool wouldn't listen."

"Is Bob your husband?"

"The radio said it was the worst hurricane ever. Worse than Camille or Katrina or Andrew. The worst one ever. They called it Atlas. We moved down here from Albany. We wanted to go where it was warm and Bob could play golf all year round. Bob was terrible at golf, but he loved to play. We sold the Honda dealership. Now all my things are gone."

I ran my tongue over my dried and cracked lips. "Where is Bob now?" I really didn't want to know the answer. "Was he hurt in the explosion?"

"Are you a prophet?" The woman's swaying increased its rhythm. "You're an older man. Tall as a tree. You have wild white hair. You must be a prophet. After the apocalypse, the prophets will come and take us to a better place."

"No. I'm not a prophet. I live across the highway in a beach house. Or at least I did. I ran over here when the big wave came. My house washed away." I shook my head. "We need to find your husband. Or someone who can help you. Us. I need help too."

"It's the punishment of the Lord," the woman said in her emotionally vacant voice.

"Let's see if we can find some help."

"And the rains came and the winds of His vengeance blew as never before."

"Okay, I said. "What'd you say we discuss all this later? Right now, I need to find Bob or the police or some rescue workers or somebody who can lend us a hand." I looked around the desolate landscape. Finding help looked like a tall order.

"I don't know what to do. Bob always knows what to do."

"There's an office building behind me," I said. "That's where I waited out the storm surge. Maybe you could wait in there while I go and find help. How does that sound?"

The woman looked at the financial services offices and managed a nod.

I took her arm and led her back to the flooded office. She was like a child. I fixed up a place for her to sit in the back of the office and she sat quietly in an executive chair with her hands folded in her lap.

"I'll be back as soon as I find help," I said. "Just sit tight and wait for me. No more wandering around. Okay?"

The woman managed another nod.

I slung my pack over my shoulder and went back out into the wasteland, scanning the sky in the hope that a rescue helicopter might appear. No such luck.

After crossing the flooded highway, I scrambled over the top of one of the few remaining dunes to survey the landscape. Before I could even locate where I was, my cellphone went off. The barking dogs sounded harsh and out of place.

I jerked the phone out of my pocket. "Hello. Hello."

The voice on the other end sounded faint and far away. "Bugs! Help!" It was Skylar.

"Where are you Skylar?"

Static assaulted my ears. "Help. . . we tried. . . everything flooded."

"Speak up, darling. I can barely hear you. Is Rand with you?" The reception disintegrated into a series of electronic crackles and hums. I pressed the receiver tighter against my ear.

"Rand. . . hit his head. . . where is Mom?"

"I don't know," I said. "Calm down, honey. Where exactly are you guys?"

"Bugs! We tried. . . please help us. Hurry."

"Where are you!" I shouted into the phone.

Whatever Skylar said faded into a curtain of static and buzzing.

I felt heartbroken, not to mention scared. I looked around me. I had never felt so helpless in my whole life. I exhaled a deep breath and punched Susan's number into the phone. Another static storm. I was on my own.

CHAPTER 18

I STUMBLED OVER THE TOP of the dune and below me I saw the access road that ran past my house. Overturned cars littered the road, all of them heavily salt stained. Fallen trees had crushed two of them.

I hiked down to the first one and peered in the driver's side. A young man lay slumped over the steering wheel, his face covered with blood, probably from a broken nose.

He was dead.

His skin was gray and his unseeing eyes stared out at the turbulent waves of the Gulf. I had seen dead bodies in Vietnam, but I never got used to the sight. The young man's life was over long before it should have been. The thought left me empty and sad.

I followed the access road until I reached what remained of my beach house. It wasn't much. The porch and the back of the house that faced the Gulf were gone and the left side of the house had collapsed. There was nothing left but a shell.

A trip around the rubble left me with mixed feelings of fear, sadness and panic. The water in what remained of the house was knee deep and recognizable objects—chairs, DVDs, my coffee pot—bobbed around in the muddy mess.

I snapped out of my reverie. I didn't have time for self-pity. Skylar and Rand and Bob's wife and probably Susan were in a bad spot and it was up to me to find help for them.

Fortunately, the roof of my carport was only partly ripped away. The Town Car was caked with salt. I found a hoe in the carport and chiseled the salt off the front windshield, tossed my backpack in the passenger side and slide into the driver's seat.

I had grabbed my keys on the way out of the house. Some habits die hard.

But the Town Car refused to start. I turned the key, pumped the accelerator, said a prayer and cussed like an old army ranger but the Lincoln wasn't going to take me anywhere. The storm had flooded the engine.

I pounded the steering wheel in frustration.

The pain in my hip had reached the point it needed attention, so I dug around in my pack, found my biggie sized bottle of ibuprofen and washed down four tablets with a hearty swig from one of my bottles of water. I wanted to stay off the industrial strength pain meds as long as I could because they left me groggy. I was hungry and wolfed down a chocolate peanut butter power bar.

Now it was time to saddle up and ride.

There had to be cops or national guardsmen or Red Cross people or somebody that could save the kids. Not to mention the poor woman back at the strip mall financial office. Maybe they could even help me find Susan.

I abandoned the Town Car, slung my backpack over my shoulder and headed back for the highway, limping like mad, waiting for the ibuprofen to kick in.

My best bet was to head north on Highway 72 and then take Florida Avenue west toward the Bay St. Edwards downtown area. The town was further from the Gulf and might not have been hit as hard as my beach house neighborhood.

I'd spent my life hiking the Rocky Mountains and a couple of miles to downtown Bay St. Edwards seemed doable. I was also confident I'd find some cops or rescue workers along the way.

I trudged over the dunes and went back to the strip mall. The woman I had left in the financial office was gone. I silently wished her luck.

Back outside, the highway was underwater but the higher ground off the shoulder looked passable so I started walking north.

The ibuprofen still hadn't showed up, so I shifted my pack to my other shoulder to take the pressure off of my hip and slowing down helped the throbbing pain. Don't let anybody tell you different, getting old sucks.

But my grandkids were out there somewhere in the desolate landscape and needed my help, so it was time to quit bitching about everything I had lost and find out what I had left.

CHAPTER 19

THE WALK TO TOWN WAS a horror show. My hip ached and the wind blew salt spray into my eyes. I felt disoriented. There were no cars, no people. There weren't even any birds circling the sky.

Climbing over tree trunks and chunks of steel ripped from nearby buildings slowed my progress and my mood grew steadily darker. The storm reminded me of old age. No treatment. No cure.

After a mile or so, I sat down on a tree trunk that had been flung across the highway. I opened my backpack and fished out a small jar of petroleum jelly and covered the side of my toes and the underside of my feet with generous swabs of the goo. The last thing I wanted were blisters.

I resumed my lonely walk down Highway 72 and after another mile, the desolation of the landscape and the magnitude of what had happened in the last few hours got to me. I started talking out loud.

"Bay St. Edwards is further than I thought," I said. "And my hip hurts like hell. Just thought you'd like to know." I paused like I expected a reply.

"So this is what it feels like to go nuts." Still no reply.

"Maybe I'm being punished for getting myself banned from Colorado for life. Or for being such a lousy grandfather. What'd you think, John?"

A hundred yards later, the reply came. "The universe doesn't care that much about you, Coffman." The words tumbled out of my mouth. "Get over yourself."

Nothing like a nice chat.

From somewhere in the deep recesses of my brain, I heard the strains of the old Buddy Holly song, "I Guess It Doesn't Matter Anymore." Did Buddy call it, or what?

I danced away from a downed power line. Not exactly Fred Astaire but I avoided being electrocuted.

Across the highway, I saw the remains of a Shell gas station. The station was all but obliterated, but it was a landmark that meant I was only about half a mile from the Florida Avenue turn off. I was closer to civilization than I thought.

Heartened, I started walking with renewed purpose, and my spirits soared even more when I saw the cop.

His familiar black and white car with *Bay St. Edwards Police Department* on the side was parked off the highway next to the dunes. He was pulling something out of his trunk.

"Hey!" I called. "Hey. Over here. I need help." I waved and limped faster. "Hey."

The cop didn't react. Maybe he didn't hear me. But that seemed odd since I was no more than twenty yards away from him.

He wrestled a large cardboard box out of the trunk, staggering under its weight as he headed off between the dunes.

"Hey! Help!"

The cop didn't turn around.

I hobbled after him.

I was gasping by the time I got to the dunes. I felt dizzy but I followed the cop to a stretch of beach and stopped. Down below me, a few feet from the still angry waters of the Gulf, I spotted a concrete block beachcomber's house. Back in the fifties, beach bums flocked to the Emerald Coast and built the low two room shacks. They were cheap, safe and afforded a breathtaking view of the sea.

Susan and her developer friends had removed most of them in the interest of progress.

But it wasn't the beachcomber's shack that made me stop. It was the swarm of uniformed policemen wearing surgical masks and yellow rubber gloves carrying body bags from somewhere behind the shack to an enormous truck parked on the access road that lead away from the beach.

The sign of the side of the truck indicated that the vehicle was normally used to deliver refrigerated food to grocery stores and restaurants. The cops worked in pairs, each pair carried a body bag and moved from the shack to the truck with military precision.

My crazy world had taken another bizarre turn, but I forced myself to limp down the sandy slope toward a tall, tanned cop who seemed to be in charge of the whole operation.

"Please help me," I said as I approached the cop. "My daughter and my grandchildren are missing and I need---"

"What the hell are you doing here?" The cop spun around and faced me. His eyes were narrow and bloodshot. Thick stubble covered his chin. He was almost as tall as I was. Maybe in his mid-fifties with premature white hair.

"I need help," I said. "I need you to send somebody. . .

"Get out of here. Right now."

"But. . ."

"Don't give me lip, Bud. You don't belong here. This is police business. Leave now. You understand me?"

I couldn't believe what I was hearing. "But you're the police. My grandchildren could be in real danger."

"Look, Gramps," the cop said, glaring at me. "We're here on police business. There may be some Red Cross people in town. Maybe they can help you."

"That's insane," I said.

"Move on, you old coot." The cop had a gold name tag below his badge that read "Brunson."

"Officer Brunson, please. . ."

"It's Chief Brunson and this conversation is over. You can't imagine the crap going down around here. We've just been through the worst hurricane in human history. We've got hundreds of dead bodies. If those kids are still alive count your blessings. We can only take care of one thing at a time." His voice was strained "Take a hike." Chief Brunson turned his back on me.

I was too stunned to move.

With each passing minute, the world made less and less sense. I was looking at a dozen police officers and my grandchildren and my daughter were god knows where, facing all kinds of dangers. What kind of logic called for helping the dead before the living?

Chief Brunson whirled around. His face was a mask of anger. He drew his pistol and aimed it at my chest. "Move it, Gramps. And I mean now."

I opened my mouth but realized more words would be a mistake. Instead I turned around and staggered back up the sandy hill, passed the sandbanks and back to the highway. What the hell was going on? How could there be that many dead people in a beachcomber's shack? What were the cops doing? Why wouldn't they help me?

I hoisted my backpack over my shoulder and started back down the center of the highway. The smell of salt and seaweed made me gag. Damned Florida. The water had receded and the middle of the road was easier than walking on the sandy shoulder. I felt the asphalt beneath a half a foot of water.

My feet were soaked but I was close to Florida Avenue, which meant I was closing in on downtown Bay St. Edwards. Maybe Chief Brunson was right. Maybe there were Red Cross people in town. Or rescue teams from FEMA. Maybe there would be someone there who could help me find my family.

CHAPTER 20

"IT'S THE END OF THE world, Bro. We might as well enjoy it." Joel Collins tossed a tiny blue pill in his mouth and dry swallowed it.

Calder laughed. "Party hardy."

The twins slogged through a foot of salty, filthy water that led down the middle of Florida Avenue.

"And, if I read my GPS right, this little piece of crap on the map is called Bay St. Edwards," Joel said.

"Looks like as good a place as any for the world to end," Calder said. "I guess our job is to have some fun while we still can."

"Let's have breakfast first," Joel said. "I'm starved. How about that Chateau de Seven Eleven across the road over there?"

"Where the gourmets meet to eat." Calder laughed. He pulled a small pill box from the pocket of his designer slacks, opened it and removed an oblong white capsule. He swallowed the pill and grinned. "The breakfast of champions."

It was Joel's turn to laugh.

They sloshed through the water to the convenience store, their long black coats billowing behind them. The front door was undamaged, but refused to open more than a couple of inches when Joel pushed on it.

“Give me a hand,” he said.

Calder stepped back and clapped his hands.

“Very funny. First time I ever heard that one.”

Calder laughed and threw his shoulder into the door. With both men pushing, the door slowly yielded. What was blocking the door was a dead body. A white-haired man, who lay face down in a foot of water, his hair billowing outward.

“Musta drowned,” Calder said. “Tough titty.”

“There’s another one back here,” Joel said, moving into the interior of the store. “Back wall collapsed. Crushed the dude.”

Calder peered over his brother’s shoulder at the body of an Asian man whose unseeing eyes stared at the ceiling as dirty water lapped his face.

“It’s the apocalypse, Bro. I’m telling you.” Joel said. “The end of the world is upon us.”

“Amen, Brother Joel,” Calder said. “Let’s eat.”

“Sounds like a plan.”

Calder surveyed the grocery shelves. “We’re in luck,” he said. “Cheetos. My favorite.” He tossed a bag to Joel and ripped open another one. He shoved the crunchy snacks into his mouth as fast as he could.

Joes tore open his own bag. “Let the feast began.”

The brothers wandered around the store, sampling assorted snack food, taking a few morsels from each package and then tossing the remains on the watery floor.

At the rear of the Seven Eleven, Joel opened the refrigerator door and grabbed a quart bottle of beer. He unscrewed the cap and took a long swig. "Ah, warm beer," he said. "The champagne of the lower classes."

"You think that asswipe back at the strip club is dead yet?" Calder said, munching potato chips and washing them down with beer.

"Who cares?" Joel said. "Fucker disrespected us. No one gets away with that. Never have, never will." He ripped open a bag of pretzels. "You remember that little twerp back in New York? At the anger management group?"

"The one that said we were freaks."

"Yeah. Now that was disrespectful. Called us freaks right in front of the whole group." Joel shook his head.

"And you grabbed him and I did a number on his ugly-ass face." Calder laughed.

"And that old jerk that was running the group tried to stop you."

"So you punched his lights out."

"Damn straight. Nobody disrespects us. Nobody."

The brothers exchanged a solemn fist bump.

They drank more beer, washing down more pills.

"Let's be on our way," Calder said. "Find some fun before the world ends."

"Dancing through the apocalypse," Joel said.

They kicked the dead body that was blocking the door to the side and made their way back to the streets of Bay St. Edwards.

JOEL AND CALDER COLLINS WERE the scourge of New York's upper West Side. They descended from old, old money. Manhattan real estate, banking, blue chip stocks. The family owned a grand apartment in the city and a mansion in the Hamptons plus an apartment in Paris and an elegant beach house on the Gulf at Crystal City.

The twins were the children of older parents. An unwanted surprise. As children, they were shuffled off to a variety of boarding schools and summer camps until they were fourteen.

At which point everything changed.

The twins' father was savagely mugged outside a West Side eatery. Their mother witnessed the beating. The muggers took their father's wallet and their mother's jewelry. Their father died in the hospital a few hours later.

The muggers were never caught.

The twins' mother went into a permanent state of withdrawal. She never left her room and the twins were on their own. They brooded and sulked. Then they turned violent. Booted from two prestigious eastern prep schools, they wound up in a ritzy school for troubled children in upstate New York.

A math teacher at the school called Calder a dimwit and after class, Joel and Calder cornered the teacher in his deserted classroom and beat him to a pulp. They put a knife to his throat and threatened to harm his pregnant wife if he told anyone.

The teacher resigned the next day and moved to Michigan.

The twins tried a semester of college but got expelled, accused of trafficking in pot and prescription drugs. Not to mention sexual assault at a wild party in the Hamptons. The family lawyer got the charges dismissed.

The twins' psychiatrist told the family lawyer that both of them were sociopaths, lacking a sense of right and wrong. The lawyer, who had known the twins their whole life, agreed.

When they turned 21, the trust left to them by their grandfather kicked in and Joel and Calder were free to pursue pleasure for the rest of their lives.

They lifted weights until they were buff but not muscle bound, sported expensive haircuts and wore designer clothes and became mainstays at posh Manhattan clubs and parties. They drank heavily and inhaled a variety of drugs.

Every year they went to the family beach house in Crystal City for a few weeks of fun in the sun. The twins' psychiatrist warned that this was a titanic mistake, arguing that, unchecked and out of their normal environment, Joel and Calder could become a real menace to the people around them.

CHAPTER 21

THE WATER ON THE ROAD covered Joel's ankles and the smell of fish and decay make him gag. When he and his brother reached the center of Bay St. Edwards they were disappointed. The town was deserted.

The hurricane had slammed cars and boats into buildings and hurled benches from the town square through store windows.

"Smells like somebody's outhouse," Joel said.

"You got that right. Listen, dude, this walking crap is getting old," Calder said. "We gotta get us some wheels."

"Easier said than done." Joel surveyed the abandoned town. "Cars are going to flood in this much water. Like the 'Vet last night. Water gets under the hood and it's a no go."

The Corvette had stalled on a side road heading into Bay St. Edwards and the twins had broken into an abandoned house, waiting out the storm in the basement, popping pills by the handful to stay calm.

"You got any better ideas?"

Joel did a 360 turn and stopped. "As a matter of fact, I do. Look over there."

Calder looked where his brother was pointing.

They stared at the sign over a shop that read: "Mike's Motorcycles. Kawasaki, Honda. Used Bikes."

"Cool, dude. A couple of bikes would be awesome," Calder said.

"Then what are we waiting for?"

Mike's Motorcycles had missed the brunt of the hurricane. One window had blown out and sand had piled up around the front of the building, but otherwise the place looked solid.

In contrast, the hurricane had reduced several buildings on the same block to rubble. Massive bombing couldn't have done more damage.

Calder tried the front door of Mike's Motorcycles but it was locked. He picked up a stray brick from a pile that had once been the building next door and heaved it through the plate glass window. The sound of shattering glass echoed through the quiet of the deserted town. He reached inside the jagged hole and unlocked the door. "After you."

Joel stepped into the store.

To his right, a row of shiny Honda motorcycles had been crushed by a collapsed ceiling beam. On the left, a pair of rebuilt, 3-wheel ATVs sat apart like a couple of outcasts.

Water poured from a hole in the ceiling where the beam had been, adding inches of water on the floor. There were no lights and the shop stank of mildew and sewage.

The sound of a radio echoed from the back of the shop.

. . .coastal area has received over 50 inches of rain in the last 24 hours. The governor has declared a state of emergency. Hurricane Atlas. . . most destructive storm in over a hundred years.

Calder sat in the saddle of one of the ATVs, gripping the handlebars and mimicking revving up the machine. "Rumm. . . Rumm. . . . Rumm."

"These babies would get us anywhere." Joel hovered over another ATV.

"What the hell do you boys think you're doing?"

Joel swiveled around on the ATV.

A man appeared from an alcove in the back of the bike shop and leveled a shotgun at Joel's midsection.

Calder stopped in mid-rumm.

"Radio warned us to watch out for looters," the man said. "Punks like you think you can come in here and help yourself to my stock. Well, think again, boys. I'm Mike and this is my shop."

The man looked like he hadn't slept in days. His eyes were rimmed red and his chin was covered in stubble.

"No sir," Joel said. "That was certainly not our intention."

"Shut your yap." Mike had a tic that made the right corner of his mouth continually twitch as he spoke. "I know looters when I see them. You two are awfully well dressed to be out stealing bikes but I reckon looters come in all shapes and sizes."

"No, really." Joel held up his hands in a gesture that said 'don't shoot.' "We were looking for help. We got caught in the storm last night. Out phones went out. We're from out of town. We were scared."

"We're all scared, son," Mike said. "We all just went through hell. Goddamn hurricane came out of nowhere. All that Doppler shit didn't see it coming."

Joel nodded, encouraging the man to keep talking, hoping it would take his mind off the shotgun.

"A Cat5 hurricane," Mike said. "Never thought I'd see one. They call the sonofabitch 'Atlas'. Ain't that a name? He shook his head. "Left dead folks all over town."

"Yeah. We found a couple of bodies at a convenience store on the edge of town. Looks like you were smart." Joel's eyes searched the store for some kind of weapon. "Boarded up the windows. Great idea."

"This place is all I got," Mike said. "That and my navy pension."

Calder's eyes drifted to the ignition of the ATV. The key was in it. He let a loud, maniacal cackle.

Mike swung the shotgun around. "What's your problem, son? Are you simple minded? This ain't no time to be laughing."

Calder frowned. The simple-minded crack had been a slap in the face. All of his life people had been saying stuff like that about him. In the apocalypse, he didn't have to take it. If the world was coming to an end, there was no rulebook, no law. He could do whatever he wanted. He turned the ignition key. The ATV's engine surged to like. Rumm. . . Rumm. . . Rumm. For real.

"What the hell are you doing? Turn that thing off." Mike raised the shotgun to his shoulder. "Turn it off now."

Calder released the brake.

"Rumm. . . Rumm. . . . The noise overwhelmed the tiny shop.

"I said turn it off!"

Calder threw the three-wheeler in gear and gave the engine full throttle. The all-terrain vehicle bucked forward, almost throwing him off. He settled into the saddle and aimed the ATV across the store front. The vehicle surged forward, plowing into the surprised Mike before he could squeeze the trigger of the shotgun.

The weapon flew out of Mike's hand as the ATV slammed him against the counter. His head snapped back and he fell to the floor.

Calder gave the machine more gas.

Mike twisted away. He rolled a couple of feet and struggled to get to his feet.

Joel retrieved the shotgun.

Calder pivoted the ATV away from the counter and aimed it at Mike as the store owner tried to crawl away.

The ATV hit Mike full force, rode up over his body and continued on across the showroom. Calder's insane giggle echoed off the low ceiling. He wheeled the ATV around and drove it back over Mike, catching him in the face with the front wheel.

A river of blood ran from the corner of Mike's mouth. He clutched at his chest and his eyes grew wide as more blood gushed out of his ear. Then his body convulsed and went rigid.

"Well done, dude," Joel shouted above the noise of the engine. "Awesome."

Calder grinned and revved the ATV engine. He considered another pass at Motorcycle Mike but decide that would be useless since the man was clearly dead.

"I got to get me one of those." Joel approached the other all-terrain vehicle. "I think this one has my name on it." He said, jumping into the saddle.

He checked Mike's shotgun. "Locked and loaded," he said. "Two barrels. No extra ammo, but two pops from this thunder stick might come in handy."

Calder nodded his approval.

In a minute, the twins, astride their new toys, roared back out into the deserted streets of Bay St. Edwards. The howl of the engines shattered the silence. They headed west, whooping and hollering, reveling in the joy of the apocalypse.

Behind them, the radio in the back of Mike's Motorcycles continued broadcasting.

The power is out all up and down the Emerald Coast. Hundreds are believed dead. Authorities are swamped and unable to deal with the calamity. Hurricane Atlas is one for the ages.

CHAPTER 22

I WAS STILL FUMING ABOUT the cops refusing to help me, not to mention Chief Brunson pulling a gun on me, when I reached downtown Bay St. Edwards. One look at the deserted, devastated streets and disappointment replaced my anger. There was no one in Bay St. Edwards. Not a soul. No police. No firefighters, no Red Cross workers, no FEMA people. Bay St. Edwards was a ghost town.

Cars were overturned in the middle of Main Street, piles of rubble where stores had been spilled over the sidewalk. The hurricane had smashed storefront windows up and down the street, scattering glass shards all over the walkway.

Welcome to downtown Hell.

I paused in front of one of the remaining storefront windows and looked at my reflection. Who was that guy? My hair stuck out in unruly white tuffs. My skin looked more wrinkled than usual and my shoulders slumped. Age was as bad as the hurricane at taking away everything you had.

I sat on the hood of a Ford truck, whose tires had gone flat and ate a power bar, washing it down with a couple of swigs from one of my water bottles. I had read somewhere that a human being could survive on a quart of water a day. I was testing that hypothesis. I was willing to bet the local water was contaminated and I only had three bottles left in my backpack to last me, God only knew how long. It was hard to limit my intake to two or three sips. Dry mouth was becoming my constant companion.

I finally hopped off the car and walked down the south side of the downtown area. The local coffee shop was a pile of rubble. Same with the stationary store and the men's shop that featured Hawaiian shirts and Bermuda shorts.

I paused outside "Mike's Motorcycles". The storefront windows were smashed but the building remained intact. I could hear a radio playing in the back of the store. My hopes soared.

"Mike! Mike! Are you in here?" The front door was gone so I walked into the store. "Mike. It's John Coffman. Are you here? I need some help."

Mike was one of the nicest guys I'd met since moving to Bay St. Edwards. We shared a passion for college football and whenever I came to town, I made it a point to pick up a couple of lattes at the coffee shop and stop by Mike's store and catch up on the latest news about Mike's beloved Florida Gators.

There would be no news from Gator Nation today. Mike was dead.

His mangled body lay in the middle of the flooded floor, surrounded by toppled motorcycles. Half of his face was gone.

It took a couple of deep breaths to keep from tossing my power bar.

The floor of the shop was covered with mud and sand and I could make out the tracks of a couple of ATVs that had circled the interior of the store and then headed out the missing front door.

What had happened to Mike? If the store was still standing, I couldn't figure out how the storm had gotten to him. Something had done serious damage to his face and, judging from the angle of his body, broken one of his legs.

I looked at the tracks again and the truth hit me.

Somebody had killed him. Apparently, a couple of looters had tried to steal the ATVs, Mike had tried to stop them and they had killed him. Looters were common in the wake of disasters and I shook my head and fought back tears.

The voice on the radio cut through my reverie.

Rescue teams are having difficulty gaining access to several areas of the Emerald Coast. Roads are washed out, bridges have collapsed. Power lines are down. Contact with the local police has been sporadic.

"Bastards are too busy moving bodies on the beach," I said out loud.

The more I thought about it, the more ridiculous the whole thing seemed. Why weren't the police going house to house, looking for survivors? Or guarding businesses like Mike's that were still standing? Something seriously weird was going on.

I took a last look at Mike's mangled corpse. "Sorry, old friend," I said in a choked voice. "Your Gators are a lock this year to win the SEC. Wish you were going to be here to see it."

I headed back to the street. Night was coming and fatigue and dread closed in on me. A block later, my cellphone went off and I fished it out of my jeans. "Bugs. Help." Skylar's voice penetrated the curtain of static. "We're trapped in the mall. We can't get out." The flat quality of her voice told me she was in some kind of shock.

"Speak up, darling. I can barely hear you."

"The bottom floor of the mall is flooded and there are snakes everywhere. Rand hit his head and it's bleeding. I'm so scared. Please come and get us."

"I'll be there as fast as I can," I said.

"Where is Mom? Her phone doesn't answer."

"I don't know. I can't reach her either."

"Bugs. Please help us. We're trapped in this creepy Halloween store on the second floor. All the mannequins are dressed up like Star Wars characters and monsters and superheroes. I hate it. All these big chunks of metal and piles of sand are blocking the door. I tried everything but the door won't open."

"Do you have anything to eat?"

"Sorta. Rand has some candy bars. But we don't have any water and I'm really thirsty.

"Okay. Don't worry. Don't eat all of the candy bars at once. Look in the back of the store. Maybe there's some bottled water in there somewhere. It's gonna be a while before I can get there."

"No. Please. We need help now." Skylar started crying. Softly at first, then louder. I was so frustrated I wanted to cry myself.

"Stay strong, darling. I'll be there as soon as I can."

"What? I can't hear you. You're breaking up. Please, Rand is. . . " Skylar's voice faded out.

I felt like heaving the phone across the street.

Instead, I punched Susan's number. Nothing happened. Only silence.

I had never felt so helpless in my life. Mike had been murdered and my grandkids were trapped and scared in a mall several miles away. I didn't have a car. Mike's killers had taken the only two ATVs in the shop and trashed all the motorcycles. There was no one in Bay St. Edwards. The cops were less than worthless. I was on my own.

I slung my backpack over my shoulder. I would have to walk all the way to the mall. No matter what. I took a deep breath and took a step.

Through the ringing of the tinnitus in my ear, I could hear Tommy Liddell's voice. Faint, but echoing through all the years. "I'm calling your number big fellow. Don't let me down."

CHAPTER 23

"IT'S THE A POC O LYSPE!"

Joel drove his ATV through the shattered front door of the Walgreen's Drugstore on the corner of Florida Avenue and Oak Street.

"And we're gonna celebrate with Da Rugs!!" Calder crashed through the door a step behind his brother. Water stood a foot deep throughout the store and the spinning wheels of the ATVs splattered watery gunk over the stocked shelves.

Earlier, the twins had raided an abandoned army surplus store and Calder was decked out in a fatigue jacked and army field hat that he wore at an off-centered angle which make him look like a hipster Marine. A bicycle chain dangled from his right hand.

Calder sped down the broad aisle of the drugstore on the ATV, letting out a series of wild yells as he assaulted the shelves with the whip end of his bicycle chain. Lipstick, eyelash brushes, nail polish and hair brushes flew through the air.

The chain shattered bottles of moisturizer, mouth wash and shampoo. He made a sharp right turn and continued his assault along the back wall of the drugstore.

Joel perched on his ATV at the end of the aisle, shaking his head and roaring with laughter. "Dancing through the apocalypse!"

Calder's engine howled and his bike chain lashed out at the shelves. Styling tools, cans of hair spray, bottles of lotion, greeting cards and cat and dog food sailed in all directions.

Joel revved up his own engine and roared down the far aisle, using his own bicycle chain to clear the shelves of laxatives, antacids, Depends, cold and flu medicines. He stopped at the end of the aisle to help himself to a package of potato chips and a can of Red Bull.

"Dude! Back here! Check it out!" Calder's voice echoed through the cavernous store.

Joel gave his vehicle full throttle and rocketed to the rear of the store, where he found Calder, who had dismounted his ATV and was bent over a small TV set that was hooked up to a portable generator on the pharmacy counter.

The flickering screen held an image of Ned Wallace, standing in front of a colorful weather map.

"We're in deep shit, Bro," Calder said.

On the screen, Ned Wallace pointed to the map. "And down here," he said. "In tiny Bay St. Edwards, the Zephyr Bay Bridge has collapsed on the west side and over here, on Highway 72, giant sinkholes have put the road out of operation."

"That's us," Calder said. "Bay St. Edwards. Damn, dude. We're trapped here. Look at that. They can't get any cars or trucks or anything in here. The whole peninsula is sealed off. No state cops, no national guard, no rescue people."

"No rules, no law," Joel said with a grin. "We can do anything we want. And I mean anything."

"Cool."

Ned Wallace stared into the camera. "Authorities are urging any survivors in the Bay St. Edwards area to hold on as best you can. We're forecasting more bad weather for the entire Emerald Coast. But you people hang on out there. As soon as there's a break in the weather, the national guard is going to try to land helicopters with rescue teams up and down the coast, but they have to wait until the wind dies down. So hang on." A big smile appeared on the weatherman's face. He adjusted his earpiece and the smile vanished.

"Gotta raise hell while we can, dude," Joel said.

"You got that right," Calder said. "And look where we're standing. Smack in the middle of a DRUG store. How great is that?"

"Party on, bro."

Joel hurdled the pharmacy counter with the skill of an athlete, while Calder crawled over the counter with far less agility.

"Oh, shit," Joel wailed. "What a bummer. Check it out."

Calder looked where his brother was pointing. In the back of the pharmacy, an entire wall had collapsed and rows of shelving had toppled over and lay in two feet of murky water. All of the pharmacy stock was either floating in the water or had sunk to the bottom of the filthy flood.

"Sonofabitch." Calder slammed his fist down on the counter. "I'm running low, bro. We need to find some stuff fast."

Joel shook his head. "I'm running low myself. Let me think." He pressed his palms against the wall and stared down into the murky water. "Wait a minute," he said. "When we drove through this burg last year, I got a speeding ticket. Remember? It wasn't too far from here. You remember what was across the road from where I got pulled over?"

Calder looked like his brother had asked him to explain quantum physics.

"The big mall. Remember? The Emerald Something Mall. There was a sign in front. One of the box stores was a Drug Rite. Remember?"

"Kinda."

"Drug Rite is inside the mall. All the drugs we could want. Right there. I can't believe I didn't think of it earlier. Come on, man. It's just a few miles from here. Acres and acres of little blue babies and Oxycottons and Vikings. All we could want. Damn, Bro. What are we waiting for? Let's go."

A couple of minutes later, the twins roared out of Walgreen's on their ATVs, dancing into the apocalypse.

CHAPTER 24

TWO HUNDRED YARDS ON THE far side of downtown Bay St. Edwards, Florida Avenue became impassable. A giant sinkhole had swallowed up a football field worth of asphalt and water had flooded in, forming a tiny lake. The earth on either side of the highway had cracked and buckled.

There was no way around the hole.

A side road veered off to the south. I wasn't familiar with that part of town, but I figured somewhere down the road I could find a way to turn back westward and resume my journey to the Emerald Fields Mall.

The road south was swampy and I worried about alligators. When you spend a lifetime in Colorado and then move to Florida you always worry about alligators. Looking at the swampy moonscape that stretched in front of me, alligators seemed like a real possibility.

Darkness closed in, which was also a real concern since my night vision wasn't what it used to be.

Panic and frustration double teamed me. Who was I kidding? I was way past my prime, with a bum hip, and yet I thought I could hike across a hurricane-devastated stretch of Florida coast and rescue my grandchildren. The ridiculousness of that idea staggered me.

I limped down the dark, swampy road for a while, until fatigue ambushed me with a vengeance. My hip ached and throbbed and my chest felt tight. Visions of rescue workers finding my body on the side of the road taunted me. Maybe I really had stayed too long at the party.

As I shuffled down the darkening road, it occurred to me this was the logical conclusion of the events of the last few years. I had taught history at West Haven Academy outside of Denver for nearly 35 years. The kids were great, I loved history and living in the shadow of the Rocky Mountains was one step away from heaven.

Then things changed. Slowly at first, then faster and faster. The change started with my hip.

The pain wasn't bad at first. Some soreness after a handball match. Then some sharp pain coming down from climbing a fourteener. The doctor said it was nothing to worry about. Take a couple of ibuprofen.

But the pain got worse. Handball became torture. Skiing was out of the question. Hiking became a memory. They did surgery but the operation was less than a success. The pain came back worse than before.

I couldn't walk fifty yards without triggering an agony I had never known. I started to limp. The ex-fullback of the Northern State Wildcats had to throw in the towel. No more handball. No more mountain hiking or skiing. I looked up one day and said, "where did my life go?"

Megan said I had to change with the times but my bitterness grew. Change became my mortal enemy. I gripped all the time. Every little thing pissed me off.

I let Megan know the level of my misery. Everyday. In every way.

But she paid me back.

NOW I WAS THE LAST man alive in Bay St. Edwards, limping down a deserted road as night fell, desperately trying to find a way to rescue my grandchildren.

A few houses still stood on the side of the road although most of them were in bad shape. The hurricane had shattered the windows or ripped off the roofs. Trees were uprooted and dropped on the tops of garages. The backyards had become sewage filled lakes and the stench made me gag.

Darkness posed a growing problem. With the power out, there was nothing to offer illumination. The world was turning into a black hole. The sky offered a big nothing since low clouds blocked the moon.

Plus, I had to admit I was lost. The hurricane had rearranged the whole world. I hadn't found a cutoff that might send me back to Florida Avenue and the way I knew would lead me to the Emerald Fields Mall.

Exhaustion taunted me. The possibility of not reaching the kids until morning became a reality. My brain frantically searched for another way but I came up empty. When I looked at the side of the road, I saw shadows move. Alligators. Snakes. Panthers.

Then I trudged to the top of a ridge and saw a glimmer of hope. A highway, which I assumed was the Zephyr Bay Parkway, crossed over the road I was traveling. Under the viaduct, where the roads crossed, I saw a small fire burning. There were people gathered around the fire.

Maybe I wasn't the last man left in Bay St. Edwards after all.

CHAPTER 25

"WHERE THE HELL IS NED?" Barbara Stanhope nervously paced back and forth in the control room, glancing down at the weather set below. "We've got to get back on the air this morning. We're the news of the day."

Ronnie Crow looked up from his computer screen. He wasn't sure if his boss wanted an answer or was just posing a rhetorical question. He had stayed at the studio all night and his brain was still battling the fog of sleep.

"We need to get him back on the air at the top of the hour," Barbara said. "The storm is getting out of control. We've had a flood of calls."

Ronnie took a sip from his coffee cup. "Thanks again for the coffee, Miss Stanhope," he said. "That was really nice of you to bring me a cup. No one has ever done that before." He hoped the comment might distract Barbara from Ned's tardiness.

His plan worked. Barbara turned and smiled at him. "You're more than welcome. I don't know what we would have done last night without you and your computer. Ned doesn't know his ass from a hole in the ground about this stuff. Where are we now, by the way?"

Ronne couldn't take his eyes off of Barbara Stanhope. The gentle curve of her breasts, the round firmness of her rear end, the radiant smile that seemed to light up the control room. She was everything he had ever. . .

"Ronnie?"

"Oh. Sorry. I guess I'm still sleepy."

"So, tell me what's going on."

"Okay." Ronnie looked back down at his computer screen. "It's not good. I can tell you that. The first wave has already hit the Emerald coast and now Atlas is picking up incredible speed as it gets closer to land and it's on a collision course just south of here."

"The Bay St. Edwards area, right?"

"Right. I'm sure those people down there are already having a rough time. The winds are up over 90 miles per hour. In a matter of minutes, they're going to get flattened." Ronnie took a sip of his coffee. "We'll have to wait until the full force hits, measure the property damage and the death toll, but yeah, right now it looks pretty bad."

"Tell me what 'bad' would be."

Ronnie sighed. "Well, okay. In terms of damage, Hurricane Katrina was the costliest storm in our history. It did something like a hundred and twenty-five billion dollars' worth of destruction. But Katrina was a Cat 5."

"Is Atlas anywhere near that?" Barbara asked, struggling to keep the anxiety out of her voice.

"It's heading that way."

"Oh, shit."

"My sentiments exactly." Ronnie tapped a couple of keys on his keyboard. "Okay. That's what I thought. In 1969 Hurricane

Camille had measured winds up to 190 miles per hour and, in terms of human life, the deadliest Atlantic hurricane was Hurricane Mitch back in 1998. It killed over 11 thousand people."

"But there's not much chance of something like that happening again, right?"

"We can only hope."

"Damn. This stuff is depressing," Barbara said.

"If you get outside the United States, it only gets worse," Ronnie said. "In 1931 an unnamed hurricane in the Western Pacific took over 300,000 lives and Hurricane Nina in 1975 killed around 26,000 people in China."

"Let's keep our fingers crossed," Barbara said.

Ronnie looked back down at this computer and tapped a few more keys. "Oh, no. Miss Stanhope. Look at this."

Barbara looked over Ronnie's shoulder at the screen.

"You remember that swirling purple mass I showed you and Mr. Wallace last night? Check this out. It's turned red. Look. Right there in the northern Gulf." He pointed at the spot on the screen "Dark red. That's something the meteorology professors only talk about. It's not supposed to really happen."

Barbara leaned forward and squinted at the screen. "What's that little spur right there?" She put her finger on the screen.

"Oh, God," Ronnie said. "The storm's already reached land. Its. . . . Its already touched down right on top of Bay St. Edwards."

CHAPTER 26

FOUR PEOPLE SAT HUDDLED AROUND a small fire under the viaduct—a man and two women, along with a small boy, who couldn't have been more than five or six.

"Hello," I called as I approached the encampment.

The man leaped to his feet and glared at me with a combination of fear and anger. He clutched and unclutched his fists.

"Relax," I said. "I'm not bent on doing anybody any harm. The storm's done enough of that already."

The man's shoulders sagged and his hands dropped, although I could tell he was still on danger alert. He was in his mid-forties with thick, dark hair and a unibrow. He wore a plaid shirt and a pair of designer slacks.

"It's good to see some fellow human beings," I said, holding up my hands in a gesture that indicated I meant no harm. "I thought I might be the last man left on the peninsula."

"Well, come sit down by the fire, Last Man Left.'" The woman had short, cropped bleach-blond hair with dark roots. She had kind eyes and I slid off my backpack and found a seat beside her. She smiled in greeting.

Once I sat down, I realized that I was totally exhausted. There was no more gas in the tank.

"I'm Herb Bluitt," the man said. "I'm afraid I don't even know these two ladies' names. We stumbled on each other a little while ago. I'm a software engineer at Monesco. I was working late in the lab in the basement and didn't realize how bad the storm was. By the time I left the building, the wind had slammed my BMW into a couple of other cars. Biggest mess you've ever seen."

Sitting down relieved the pressure on my hip and I had to stop myself from sighing out loud. "I'm John Coffman," I said. "I'm trying to get to the Emerald Fields Mall. I've got a couple of grandkids trapped in the upper level. The bottom half of the mall is flooded."

"That's terrible," the blond woman patted my arm. "Maybe we can help."

"You're not going to make it out there tonight," Bluitt said. "The roads are flooded. You might step on a downed power line. Not to mention alligators and God knows what other varmints might be lurking in the dark."

I exhaled a deep breath. "Every silver lining has a cloud." As much as I hated to admit it, Bluitt was right. I was so tired, I realized I was struggling to stay awake while we were talking. Standing up would be a challenge, let alone trying to hike to the mall.

"Where are the authorities?" The other woman was on the verge of tears. "We spent all day waiting for a rescue team. There was no food, no water. Bobby Joe cried the whole time." She indicated the boy.

Bobby Joe looked catatonic. He stared into the fire with unblinking eyes.

"The authorities can't get on the peninsula," Bluitt said. "The causeway collapsed last night. Route 72 is underwater. The whole peninsula is cut off. They can't even land helicopters because of the wind."

My heart sank. What was I going to do about Skylar and Rand? How was I going to find Susan? I felt dizzy.

"You okay?" the blonde put her hand on my shoulder.

"Just tired," I said. "Thanks."

"You'll get the kids," she said. "We'll figure something out."

"They've got to help us," the other woman shrieked. "They can't leave us like this. We pay taxes." She was in her mid-thirties. Her long dark hair matted and tangled and her pink sweatshirt was spotted with what looked like dried blood. There was a deep cut under her right eye.

Bobby Joe's gaze never left the fire. The kid was in a bad way.

"There were some local cops out by the Highway 72-Florida Avenue intersection," I said. "They were retrieving bodies from the beach. I tried to get them to help, but the chief said they were too busy. Seemed strange to me. The chief ran me off."

Bluitt laughed. "I'm sure you misjudged the situation," he said in a voice people saved for children and victims of dementia. "Surviving a hurricane is so far outside what we normally experience, we believe things happened that didn't."

"This happened."

Bluitt shrugged. "And given your age, it's understandable you may not be computing what's going on around you correctly."

What a know-it-all jerk off. 'Compute this, shithead' made to the tip of my tongue but didn't leave my lips. No point in getting into it with the only people on the peninsula who might be able to help me.

"I bet you ran into Chief Brunson," Bluitt said.

"Yeah. He was the guy in charge."

"Brunson's an old school cop." Bluitt sat down on the ground and warmed his hands in the heat of the fire. "Strict law and order man. He's the errand boy for the developers and the tourist moguls. Pretty rough around the edges."

"You're telling me. But why were there so many bodies on the beach? Wouldn't most people have evacuated before the hurricane hit?"

"Nothing makes sense in conditions like these. We're all living in total chaos," Bluitt said as if that explained everything.

"Yea, but it was pretty mysterious," I said. "I wanted to go back to the beach and see what the cops were up to, but I needed to get to the mall and my grandkids as fast as I could."

"You made the right choice." The blond had a husky, throaty voice.

"Out by Monesco, where I work, an office building collapsed." Bluitt's mouth apparently never ran down. "It was like a war zone. People went nuts. One guy curled up on the ground in a fetal position and kept calling for his mother. A grown man. Calling for his mama."

"You ever been in a war zone?" I asked politely.

"No."

"It's not what you think."

"Shut up! All of you! Just shut up!" The dark-haired woman burst into tears. "I don't want to hear any more. I don't want to die! Not like this! Stop it! Just stop it!"

"Take a deep breath, Annie." The blonde jumped up and cradled the hysterical woman in her arms. They rocked back and forth while Annie sobbed.

Bluitt shrugged.

Bobby Joe's eyes never left the flickering flames of the fire.

Nobody said anything for a while.

"A hurricane releases more energy every hour than an atomic bomb." Bluitt stirred the fire with a stick.

The guy was probably as scared as the rest of us and covered up his fear with constant yakking.

"Even the name comes from 'Huracan,' which was a pre-Columbian storm god. It was a wildly unpredictable deity."

I had taught students like Bluitt over the years. The smartest guy in the room.

"In an average season, we have around ten named storms. Then we have a few hurricanes that don't amount to much and maybe one major monster. A Cat3 or higher. But this thing has defied all odds. The radio is calling it a Cat5."

Annie let out a moan and the blonde shot Bluitt a look that would have withered roses.

But nothing stopped Herb Bluitt. "It actually may not be the worst. There was another one on the east coast in 1938, but it didn't get any publicity. Nobody ever heard much about it."

"Because the storm hit the day after Hitler's troops invaded Czechoslovakia," I said, hoping to close the topic.

Bluitt looked disappointed I had spoiled his punch line.

But disappointed or not, he kept trucking. “What I don’t understand,” he said. “Is why we didn’t get more warning. I mean we live in a post-industrial society with all kinds of sophisticated computers, algorithms and technology. How could they have missed it?”

I let out a long sigh. “I think it falls under the heading of shit happens.”

A smile crept in around the corners of the blonde’s mouth.

“I’m hungry,” Bobby Joe looked up from the fire.

Annie broke into sobs again. “I don’t have any food, honey. I don’t know what to do.”

“I got you covered, partner.” I dug around in my backpack and pulled out one of my power bars. Vanilla Almond. I tore off the wrapping and handed the bar to Bobby Joe. He devoured the power bar in three quick bites. Then he went back to staring at the fire.

Annie nodded her thanks. So did the blonde.

After a while, I stretched out on the ground and used my backpack as a pillow. I closed my eyes and waves of regret washed over me. I had come up short. I didn’t make it to the mall, after I told Skylar I was on my way. I also felt a rising panic about what might have happened to Susan. The whole world felt out of control.

I forced my mind to stop the worst-case scenarios that marched across my brain like the Macy’s Thanksgiving parade. Susan was my daughter and I loved her and I couldn’t stand the thought of something horrible happening to her. Not my little girl. Not on my watch.

CHAPTER 27

THE OTHER PEOPLE SETTLED DOWN for the night, spreading out on the ground, using stray articles of clothing as blankets and purses and backpacks as pillows. The fire burned down and the night creatures serenaded us.

As tired as I felt, sleep was a no go. Bluitt snored like a malfunctioning motorcycle and periodically, Annie let out sad whimpers. Bobby Joe sat next to his mother, still staring at the fire like one of the children of the damned.

I lay in the dark, thinking about creatures that creep and crawl and slither. All of them searching for me. Or Susan. Or Skylar and Rand.

I closed my eyes and let my mind wander back to a time when the world around me made sense. I asked myself questions to find a calming peace. What were the greatest athletic performances of all time? Easy. Roger Bannister breaking the four-minute mile in 1954. Don Larson's perfect game in the 1956 World Series.

Greatest teams ever? Johnny Unitas and the Baltimore Colts of 1958. The Oklahoma Sooners under coach Bud Wilkinson, Bill Russell's San Francisco Dons. The New York Yankees with Yogi Berra and Mickey Mantle and. . .

I woke up with a start.

The fire had burned down to nothing. Herb Bluitt's snoring had leveled off and Bobby Joe had finally fallen asleep. The night bugs kept up their symphony and I resisted the temptation to grab my backpack and take off for the Emerald Fields Mall, but my Common Sense Angel whispered in my ear that that would be folly. It was too dark and I was still too exhausted.

As soon as the sun came up, I'd take off. I wouldn't let my grandchildren down. Hip or no hip, age or no age.

I thought about my students over the years. The one who won a full scholarship to Stanford. The kid who really loved history. The one who could never get her homework in on time, but aced every test. The one who was killed in a car wreck his senior year. The one. . .

Somewhere in the back of my mind I could hear the Beatles. Across the Universe. Nothing's going to change my world. Yeah, right.

When I woke up, the first rays of a muted sun peeked under the viaduct, bathing the world in a reddish glow.

The blond sat up next to me. Her eyes were open and she had her arms clutched around her knees. She looked calm. And pretty.

"G'morning," I whispered, not wanting to wake the others.

The blond turned and looked at me. Her eyes held the sadness of someone who had known their fair share of pain.

"Good morning," she whispered back.

I pulled myself into a sitting position.

"You got any coffee in that back pack?" The blond asked.

"Sorry."

She grinned. "Maybe later. I'd kill for some coffee. I don't think the local Starbucks is open at the moment."

"Not likely."

We both smiled.

I struggled to my feet. Sleeping on the ground left my body feeling like I'd been hit by a truck. "Tell you what," I whispered. "I'll get both of us a power bar and then I've got to take off. I'm going crazy thinking about what might have happened to my daughter and my grandkids."

The woman jumped to her feet. "Take me with you." She put her hand on my arm.

"What?"

"Take me with you. You're doing something worthwhile. Saving your family." She gestured to the people still sleeping under the viaduct. "They're just trying to survive. I've spent my whole life just trying to survive. If I could help you, I'd be doing something bigger and better."

"That's kind of you," I said, not sure what to make of the woman's offer.

"I know the area," she said. "I may know some shortcuts. Besides, I can't listen to Bluitt another minute. He and Annie and Bobby Joe will be fine without me."

I grinned. "Welcome aboard." I pulled a couple of power bars out of my backpack and handed one to her.

She tore into the power bar and bit off the end. "You got anything else? I don't like cinnamon nut raisin."

The broad smile on her face told me she was joking. I liked that. It was the break of dawn in a shattered, hurricane devastated world and the woman was making jokes. I liked that a lot.

She stuck out her hand. "I'm Jackie Marsh," she whispered. "Let's hit the road."

CHAPTER 28

"I FEEL LIKE WE'RE STRANDED on Mars," Jackie said, surveying the road in front of us. "Nothing looks familiar. Even the sky looks strange."

She was right. I looked up at a thick mass of gray swirling clouds. Raindrops pelted our faces.

We started the morning moving away from the viaduct campsite by walking on the side of a backstreet that carried us westward. But the going got tough almost immediately. We began to sink into the spongy, sandy earth.

The street was underwater, but it provided steadier footing than the shoulder. My feet were soaked through my boots. My stomach growled and my hip ached.

"Don't worry," Jackie said. "If your grandkids can hold on until about noon, we should be at the mall by then."

"I just hope we're not too late." I pulled out my phone but all the little bars had vanished and a dim message let me know the stupid thing had run out of power.

"If I remember correctly," Jackie said. "This street parallels Florida Avenue and then cuts north which should put us in sight of the mall."

I found Jackie's confidence reassuring.

"Put the phone up," Jackie said. "It's dead. Get over it. We'll get to the mall as soon as we can."

I stuffed the phone back in my pocket. "Damned cellphones," I said. "I used to enjoy conversation over a glass of wine at dinner or a couple of beers at the local bar or a cup of coffee at the coffee shop. I loved to talk about sports or politics or history or just gossip."

"Sure," Jackie said. "Who doesn't?"

"Then everyone started talking about their cellphone." I patted the phone in my pocket. "They talked about what apps they had or what apps they intended to get. What the apps did. Then they started shoving photos on their phone in my face."

Jackie shrugged. "Life in the 21st century."

"At some point they started texting and reading their email and surfing the web while we talked. Punching and swiping. Everybody got addicted to their little phone."

"Don't think we'll have that problem around here," Jackie indicated the drab landscape around us. "You have my full attention." She smiled.

I shook my head. I was treating Jackie the way I used to treat Megan before everything blew up. Bitching and gripping and whining and complaining. Maybe that was why God gave us old men. So we could point out everything that was wrong in the world.

How could Jackie be so hopeful? We were trudging through a junkyard world where destruction and desolation had proliferated until there was nothing left that wasn't broken, disintegrated or abandoned. Including me. I caught myself before I shared that bit of wisdom with my new traveling companion.

"What did you do before the world ended?" Jackie zipped up her denim jacket to ward off a stiff breeze that was attacking from the Gulf.

"You don't have to make nice to get my mind off the kids," I said. It came out more snappish than I had intended.

"And I thought you were going to be an improvement over that blow hard Bluitt." Jackie shot me an impish grin. "But you're just as crabby as he was. What is it with you older guys? Gripe, gripe, gripe. If you keep talking like that you'll miss all the good stuff."

I looked around the desolate landscape. The good stuff? There wasn't any good stuff. Then I looked at Jackie's smile. Maybe there was some good stuff. "Sorry," I said. "I guess I'm just worried about Rand and Skylar."

"With good reason," Jackie said. "But you and I are doing everything we can to help them. Whatever is gonna happen is gonna happen."

"I guess losing control scares the hell out of me. The hurricane. Old age. It feels like it's all getting away from me." I tried not to grimace as pain shot through my hip.

"I know what you mean," Jackie said. "But sometimes I wonder if we really have as much control over our lives as we think we do. Sometimes life seems to happen and we have to do the best we can with it."

"Like now."

"Exactly. Like now."

Jackie was right. Life did just happen. Certainty was never guaranteed. If you embraced certainty, you'd wind up in the nut house.

"To tell you the truth," Jackie said. "I'm having a weird reaction to this whole thing. The hurricane, the aftermath, life as we know it destroyed. Maybe I'm in shock, but I find it. . . I dunno. . . kind of. . . exhilarating."

"You're kidding."

"No really. It's like everything is gone, but I'm still here. I'm still alive. Everything has changed. Maybe my old life blew away with the hurricane. I'm free to start over. Free to reinvent myself, be a different kind of person. Free to do anything I want. Even something worthwhile. Like help you save. . . . what are their names?"

"Rand and Skylar."

"Yeah. Rand and Skylar. I feel like Dorothy in Oz. I'm off to have an adventure."

"You wouldn't have helped me in your old life?"

"Not likely."

"What'd you do in your old life?"

"I asked you first," Jackie said.

"High school teacher. History. A lotta years."

"Around here?" Jackie looked around and shook her head. "I mean what used to be here."

"In Colorado. That's where I'm from. I moved down here a few months ago. Old geezer retiring to Florida. I'm a walking cliché."

"You're not that old."

"Old enough to know the best part is long since over," I said.

"Get outta here. How can you get up every morning thinking that way? Even when your life is crappy, there's always a chance it'll get better."

"Yeah, but in my case, I keep looking for a few more magic moments, but they get fewer and fewer and farther and farther apart."

"Only if you quit looking."

Jackie's optimism made me ashamed of myself. She had obviously seen some hard roads in her life. At least I was still alive. Had I sunk into the abyss of geezer self-pity?

"Colorado? That sounds so romantic. Cowboys and snow-capped mountains and buffaloes," Jackie said.

And rich bastards who steal your wife, I thought. Yep, no question about it. I was knee deep in self-pity. No point in slinging it all over Jackie. "You're right," I said. "Colorado is a great place. I miss it every day."

Jackie nodded. "I've never been there. Hell, I've never been anywhere. I came down here from the Midwest years ago and just, sorta stayed. But I'd love to see Colorado. Are you a Broncos fan?"

"Sure. Everyone in Denver follows the Broncos."

"I like the Buccaneers. I watch all of their games on TV. Pro football is fun. It's a small thing, but it gives you something to look forward to every week."

"Good point."

"I like old movies too," Jackie said. "Paul Newman, Robert Redford, Dustin Hoffman, Harrison Ford. Something else fun to look forward to at the end of a hard week."

Just thinking about football and movies made me feel better. Jackie was amazing. "I love the movies too," I said. "*Butch Cassidy* is my favorite. That and *The Sting*. I can watch those movies over and over."

"There you go. They may be small, but they're still magic moments."

Shooting the breeze with Jackie was therapeutic. It took my mind off of the enormity of our mission. Not to mention the nagging pain in my hip.

We trudged past a cluster of trees that had been stripped by the wind. Jackie pointed out some sea turtles' nests and a grove of palm and palmetto trees where the mosquitoes swarmed so thick that they formed dark, quivering shapes the size of NFL linebackers.

"You'll make it to Colorado someday," I said. "Like you said. Life's an adventure. Anything can happen."

"That's the spirit," Jackie laughed. "No more of this old geezer talk."

I grinned back at her. To say I liked Jackie Marsh would have been a major understatement.

JACKIE KNEW SHE WAS DOING it again. The toxic positivity. Maybe she was doing it to hide how scared she felt. Maybe she was doing it because she genuinely liked John Coffman, crabby as he might be. Maybe it had become her fallback position.

But she also had a sneaking suspicion that it was working. She was keeping her companion's spirits up and that seemed like a very good thing.

CHAPTER 29

LATER THAT SAME MORNING, THE moonscape that had been Bay St. Edwards got worse and worse. The twins maneuvered their ATVs around downed trees and shattered blocks of concrete. Overturned cars cast eerie shadows up and down what was left of the road. Small electrical fires lit up the landscape like campfires.

They throttled past a pair of pick-up trucks that were burned out wrecks. Three decapitated bodies decorated the shoulder of the road.

The sight filled Joel and Calder with exhilaration. Calder pulled his ATV beside his brother and the twins exchanged knowing grins. All the rules, all the regulations were gone. There were no more modes of expected behavior. Civilization was a memory. No teachers, no bosses, no cops, no bouncers.

After skirting a giant sinkhole on the west side of town, the twins cut north to the Zephyr Bay beach. They passed a row of high sand dunes on the right. The incessant rain had left the dunes dark and compressed. Any foliage that had once grown around the dunes had been swept away.

As they thundered down the road, Joel spotted something moving on the beach area beyond the dunes. He slowed his vehicle and signaled his brother to turn around. They pulled the ATVs off the road and Joel pointed to someone moving between two high sand banks. The brothers grinned at each other and revved up their engines.

They roared to a stop in front of a man and a woman. Then something moved behind the woman. It was a small boy.

Beyond the beach, the dark waters of the bay swirled and crashed on the shore.

The man approached the ATVs. At first, he looked at the twins with apprehension, but then his face broke into a broad grin. "Thank God, you made it," he said. "The radio reported no rescue people could get on the peninsula." He looked a Calder's military fatigues and field hat. "What are you guys, army? National Guard?"

Joel suppressed a smile. "Something like that."

Calder giggled.

"My name is Herb Bluitt. I'm a software engineer over at Monesco. A project manager actually. That's Annie and Bobby Joe back there. We joined forces right after the hurricane subsided. Nothing but the clothes on our backs. I figured that radio report about first responders not being able to get on the peninsula was bullshit. And here you are."

"Yep," Joel said. "Here we are."

"This baby was one for the history books," Bluitt said. "I mean, shit. Look around. Everything is gone. What's your name, soldier?"

"I'm Major Wacker of the Guard." Calder snapped off a salute.

"You look awfully young to a be a major."

Calder shrugged.

"Is there anybody else around?" Joel dismounted his ATV. Calder followed suit.

"No. No one. Just us. There was another gal with us for a while. And an old guy. But they disappeared this morning. We've seen lots of dead bodies through. They're all over the place. It's horrible. I can't look at them."

Annie came up behind Bluitt. "Are you here to save us?"

"Sure," Calder said.

"So, what's the plan, Major?" Bluitt smiled at Calder.

"Have fun," Calder said with a crooked grin.

"Have fun? What are you talking about?" Bluitt looked confused.

"It's the apocalypse, dude," Joel said. "The end of the world. No more rules. No more laws. Nothing to do but enjoy yourself."

"That doesn't make any sense," Bluitt said.

Joel brought his bicycle chain out from behind his back. "Sure it does. No rules, no law. No consequences. Do whatever you like. He wrapped the bicycle chain around his knuckles. "Anything you want."

"But. . . "

"Don't argue with me Mr. Big Shot Project Manager. Not if you know what's good for you."

"I thought you guys were some kind of rescue team."

"Think again, fuckweed." Joel whipped the chain links across Bluitt's startled face.

Bluitt dropped to his knees and screamed. The chain had ripped a wide swatch of skin from the side of his face. He covered the wound with his hand, but dark red blood trickled through his fingers. "What are you. . ."

Joel lashed the bike chain across the other side of Bluitt's face. When he pulled the chain back, he could see the man's exposed cheekbone, where the skin had been ripped away. Joel kicked him in the chest and Bluitt toppled over.

"Please, stop."

Joel laughed. Then he kicked Bluitt in the ribs and then in the head. He kicked him again and again until Bluitt lost consciousness.

"It's the end of the world, you dumb asshole." Spittle flew out of Joel's mouth.

Annie's hands shot to her mouth. "What are you doing?" Her voice was approaching a scream. "Aren't you here to help us?" As the realization of what was happening dawned on her, she turned around. "Run, Bobby Joe! Run! Run down the beach!"

Bobby Joe took off.

Calder caught Annie in a few quick strides. He grabbed her by the arm and spun her around. "Let me see your tits."

"No. Please."

"Let me see your tits."

The waves crashed on the beach behind them.

"Please." The near-scream had become a whimper.

"Let me see 'em or my brother will take off your nose with his bike chain." Calder's face was locked in a crooked leer.

Behind them, Bluitt rolled over and let out an agonizing moan.

"Now!" Calder seized the front of Annie's sweatshirt and jerked it up. She wasn't wearing a bra.

"Nice. Big with big nipples. Just the way I like 'em."

When Annie tried to twist away from him, Calder slugged her in the jaw. She staggered backward. Calder followed and ripped off her sweatshirt.

"Make 'em jiggle!" Calder commanded. "Dance up and down and make 'em jiggle."

Recognizing the hopeless of her situation, Annie hopped slowly from one foot to the other. She glanced over her shoulder. Bobby Joe was gone.

"Faster!" Calder shouted.

Annie did as she was told. She fought to hold back a flood of tears but the reservoir broke and racking sobs escaped from her throat like machine gun fire.

"Now take off your pants," Calder laughed.

When Annie complied, Calder shoved her to the sandy ground. "Get on your knees, bitch!"

Annie rolled over on all fours. Calder ripped off her panties and pulled down his zipper, as she let out another scream.

She looked to the side and saw Joel striding across the sand toward she and Calder. He was unbuckling his pants and singing. "We're dancing through the apocalypse. Dancing, dancing, dancing."

CHAPTER 30

GIVEN MY BUM HIP, WE made good time, turning north and heading toward the Emerald Fields Mall. My spirits rose with each step. Despite the desolation around us, I felt like it was just a matter of time before we got to Skylar and Rand. Not too long before I found out what happened to Susan. All I had to do was keep going. One foot in front of the other. And being with Jackie Marsh was making that a lot easier.

After a half hour of steady slogging, we came to a low rise where the water in the street became shallow. We picked up our pace. "Herb Bluitt told Annie and I that a hurricane is so large, it can be seen from outer space," Jackie said.

"If anybody would know, it would be Bluitt," I said.

We both laughed and the laughter felt good.

We moved down the center of the street and, as we rounded a bend, the woodlands yielded to a small cluster of magnificent mansions at the top of the rise.

"Well, damn," Jackie said. "This is Dragon Hill. We're closer to the mall than I thought."

"What's Dragon Hill?"

"These houses are all pre-Civil War mansions but people still live in them. They run tours one Sunday every month. I went through them once. On my day off."

I opened my mouth to say something, but Jackie cut me off.

"Can you imagine what it would be like to live in a place like this?" She pointed at the nearest house, an enormous stone structure with turrets on either end and a deep porch that circled the front and side. The place was more of a castle than a house.

All the houses were set back from the road and most of them represented classic antebellum architecture with white columns that had turned gray with age. Massive oaks filled the front yards and strands of moss clung to the trees. The storm had stripped away most of the foliage, which gave the oaks a haunted, naked look.

Atlas had assaulted Dragon Hill with all of its fury. A Highlander had been hurled through the front door of one house and the roofs were missing from a couple of others.

A massive Cyprus tree had been uprooted and slammed into the house closest to the road. Rubble marked the spot where a couple of days ago, a magnificent home had stood.

Jackie stopped and rested her hands on her hips. "This is so sad," she said. "All these lovely homes."

"That one on the end looks okay," I said. "Maybe the owners evacuated in a hurry and left some food behind. You and I are going to run out of gas soon if we don't get some fuel. I'm starving." I desperately wanted to get to Rand and Skylar, but common sense told me a few minutes of foraging for food would pay big dividends on down the road.

I pushed Susan and the kids out of my mind for the time being and we headed for the house, trudging up a broad crushed gravel driveway. The place was a spacious home with a broad verandah spanning the front.

As we approached the front porch, I noticed a series of tracks in the mud in front of the stairs. Two vehicles. Three wheels each. The vehicles had come up the driveway, parked in front and then apparently left, heading back toward the main road.

The shrubbery that fronted the house was filled with debris—a mangled bicycle, some yard tools, including a chainsaw with brownish stains covering the blade, a patio chair and a detached car door.

Jackie took the lead, bounding up the front steps. I suspected she was as hungry as I was. I drug my hip up the stairs behind her.

"Watch your step," Jackie called. "The porch is swarming with snakes. The storm probably drove them out of their nests."

I froze at the top of the stairs. The verandah was alive with a squirming, wiggling mass of black snakes. "We don't see many of these in the Rockies," I said, trying not to sound too frightened.

"Just step over them," Jackie said. "I think they're king snakes. Maybe a few garden snakes. Nothing to worry about."

"What do you mean you think?"

"I'm just saying I don't see any cobras or rattlers."

I eased my way onto the verandah.

"I mean I don't think there are any."

"Thanks." I gingerly stepped over the squirming mass. The snakes barely paid me any heed.

When I reached Jackie, she grinned. "See. I told you. Life's an adventure. Hurricanes, serpents, starvation. What more could you want?"

"Speaking of starvation." I indicated the front door.

Jackie spun around and pounded on the door with the palm of her hand.

The sky grew darker and the wind picked up. A drizzling rain followed. Just another day in Paradise.

Jackie knocked on the door again.

"Nobody home," I said. "Whoever lives here probably evacuated with everyone else who had a lick of sense."

Jackie nodded. She held up a pair of crossed fingers and twisted the door knob. The door swung open.

"Wait a second," I said, fumbling through my backpack. I pulled out my flashlight. "It's a good idea to turn on the flashlight out here. If there's a gas leak in the house, the battery could spark an explosion."

Jackie nodded her approval.

I flicked on the flashlight and Jackie pushed the ancient door inward. The resulting creaking reminded me of the radio program "The Inner Sanctum" that I listened to when I was a kid. Was there really a time before TV and computers and cellphones, when we listened to the radio?

The house was cast in deep shadows and I swept the beam of the flashlight over an antique table and a wine-colored oriental rug that covered the hallway. The hall extended to the rear of the house with doors on either side.

Jackie flipped the light switch besides the front door. Nothing happened. Like the rest of the peninsula, the electricity was out on Dragon Hill.

"Hello! Hello! Anybody home?" Jackie called out in her husky voice. No one answered. "The place seems to be ours."

"Looks like."

"God, these houses are beautiful." Jackie did a 360 spin to take it all in. "You must have to store up a lot of good karma to get to live in a place like this. Living here would be heaven."

Even though I'd lived long enough to know that money was not the solution to everything, I could only wish that someday, Jackie Marsh would get to live in a house on Dragon Hill. She was a special woman.

Outside, the rain picked up.

I swung the flashlight beam into a parlor to the left of the main hallway. The room was trashed. The front windows had all blown out and shards of glass littered the hardwood floor. The rain had poured in and soaked the sofa and a pair of easy chairs, filling the parlor with the heavy smell of mildew.

As I turned around to return to the hallway, I stepped on something and lost my balance. I steadied myself on the wall but when I aimed the flashlight beam on the floor to see what I had stepped on, my stomach convulsed.

I had stepped on a human hand.

CHAPTER 31

THE FINGERS WERE LONG AND slender and the hand was a chalky gray color. Dark red tendrils extended out of the wrist.

"Are you okay?" Jackie started into the parlor.

"Stay in the hall," I said in as calm a voice as I could muster. "You don't need to see this."

Jackie froze in the doorway.

I moved away from the hand and swept the parlor with my flashlight beam. Nothing. No more body parts. I limped to the doorway, where Jackie put a hand on my arm. "Pretty bad, huh?"

"The worst." I fought back nausea. The chainsaw in the shrubbery. Surely nobody had. . .

Jackie squeezed my arm. You were sweet to protect me. That doesn't happen often. I appreciate it."

I nodded.

"Let's go find the kitchen. I'm betting it's somewhere in the back of the house," Jackie said.

My instinct was run out the front door and keep running, but if there was food in the kitchen I would hate to miss out on it.

"Okay," I said. "But be careful. Something's not right here."

As we moved down the hallway, the floorboards creaked and the mildew smell got worse. Along the way, I flashed my light into a small home office, looking for the owner of the severed hand. No luck.

On the wall, I spotted a black and white photograph of a college-aged basketball player, facing the camera, on one knee with a large grin on his face. The front of the jersey said "Duke" and the number below read "32". Judging from the kid's haircut, I guessed the photo was at least 40 years old.

Outside, the wind picked up, making the whole house groan.

At the end of the hall, we found a spacious kitchen that had recently been renovated and modernized. Stainless steel refrigerator, granite top counters. A window looked out over a smell orchard whose trees had been stripped clean. The window was cracked.

I moved the flashlight beam around the kitchen.

"Let's try that door over there," Jackie said. "I bet that's the pantry. Cover me with the light."

I guided her across the kitchen with the flashlight beam. She seized the door, yanked it open and disappeared inside.

"Jesus! John. Come here quick."

The urgency in Jackie's voice made me hustle across the kitchen.

I didn't need to hurry. Inside the pantry, two people were huddled together in a tight circle. They were dead. A man about sixty and a woman around the same age, their arms wrapped each other's shoulders like their love could save them from whatever had been menacing their mansion.

I recognized the man. I had just seen his photo in the little office. He had been number 32 at Duke decades ago.

The man was missing his left hand. The wound was draped in a white bath towel, but the towel hadn't done much good. It was soaked a deep crimson.

The powerful stench emanating from the pantry along with the grotesque swelling of their flesh left no doubt that they had been dead for a while.

"What happened to them?" Jackie took an involuntary step backward.

I remained frozen in the pantry doorway. All I could think of was Rand and Skylar trapped in the mall. What horrors could befall a pair of innocent kids in a situation like that? I put my hand on the doorsill and took a deep breath to steady myself. "It looks like somebody cut off the guy's hand and then he and the woman hid from whoever attacked them in the pantry," I said.

"That's what's in the parlor, isn't it? The man's hand."

I nodded. "My guess is these people turned on a generator so they'd have some electricity. Deadly levels of carbon monoxide can build up quickly with a generator. They can linger for a long time even after the generator has been shut down."

Jackie backed out of the pantry, unable to take her eyes off the corpses. Her face turned chalky white. "That's the saddest thing I've ever seen," she said. "I thought I'd seen the rough side of life, but this. . . this is something else."

I put my arm around Jackie's shoulder and drew her close to me. Her head sagged on my shoulder and she fought back tears.

"Let's get out of here," Jackie said after a minute, her voice muffled by my shoulder.

"Roger that."

"I'll see if there's any bottled water in the frig," Jackie said. "I know enough not to drink out of the faucet. Bacteria and all that. Could you search the pantry for something to eat. I can't go back in there."

"I'm on it."

Back in the pantry, I found an unopened jar of peanut butter, a couple of bags of almonds and a box of gourmet crackers. A feast for a king if you're hungry enough.

I avoided looking at the bodies as I stepped over them to get the food, but then a ghoulish thought crossed my mind. Maybe it wasn't so ghoulish. Maybe it would save a couple of kids' lives.

Holding my breath to combat the stench, I dropped into a catcher's crouch in front of the man's body. I moved his handless arm and stuck my hand into the front pocket of his khaki trousers.

Bingo. Americans were never without their cellphones. Even in death. This one was a smartphone and I hoped and prayed the thing didn't have a complicated password guarding it. I tucked the devise in my own pocket, sidestepped the bodies and grabbed the food off the pantry shelf. I also picked up a half empty plastic bottle of honey. Good food source that could also serve as a natural anti-septic. The rest of the shelves held nothing but canned goods.

The smell of the bodies was suffocating and the pantry generated claustrophobia. As I walked back into the kitchen, I sucked in long, deep breaths.

Outside, as suddenly as it had started, the pounding rain subsided and turned into a light drizzle.

"Let's get the hell out of here," I said. "This house is nothing but bad mojo like I've never seen."

Jackie looked relieved. "Copy that," she said. "We need to get to the mall as fast as we can and I'd rather walk in the rain than stay in here. Hell, I'd rather be doing anything that sitting around in a house with dead bodies."

I crammed the food into my backpack and Jackie and I headed for the front door.

CHAPTER 32

"HURRICANE ATLAS IS ONE OF the worst natural disasters in American history." Ned Wallace looked intently into the camera. "And folks, it's about to get worse." A slight smile crept into the corners of his mouth.

Up in the broadcast booth, Barbara Stanhope covered her face with her hands and shook her head. "Why does he do that?" she said out loud. "You don't grin like a hyena when you're delivering terrible news."

"Mr. Wallace does," Ronnie Crow said from behind his computer screen.

"Don't I know it." Barbara rolled her eyes and switched on her mic. "Go to the interview. And don't smile."

On the set, Ned blinked and went on with his report. "Our field reporter, Leslie Lomax, has a live report from near Bay St. Edwards. What have you got for us? Leslie?"

The screen to Ned's right flickered, went black and then came back on revealing a pretty young woman with dark hair, standing in front of a body of swirling water. She wore a baseball cap with a "WBEC Action News" logo on the front. She struggled against the powerful wind, one hand on her cap while the other hand held a microphone close to her mouth. The main screen went to split screen mode with Ned on the left and the field reporter on the right.

"Good evening, Ned," the girl said into the hand held mic. "I'm standing in front of what, two days ago, was the North Zephyr Causeway, the bridge that connects the western end of the Bay St. Edwards peninsula to the mainland. But less than 48 hours ago, the bridge took the full force of Hurricane Atlas, collapsed and apparently washed out to sea." The wind whipped the reporter's yellow rain slicker around her ears.

"It looks awfully rough out there, Leslie. What does all of this mean for the residents of Bay St. Edwards?"

"It means they're trapped on the peninsula, Ned. We're on the west end, across the bay and clearly no one can get to Bay St. Edwards from here and the authorities tell me that a large portion of Highway 72 on the east side has been hit by floods and sinkholes. That leaves the Bay St. Edwards' residents who didn't evacuate earlier stranded."

"What kind of efforts are being made to help those folks?"

"Well, Ned. The only possibility of help would be the national guard and their helicopters, but this fierce wind is making that a risky proposition."

As if on cue, the wind blew the reporter a couple of steps to her left.

"Have you had a chance to talk to any of the survivors?"

A puzzled look crossed the reporter's face. "Well, no," she stammered. "I'm on the north side of the causeway and the Bay St. Edwards survivors are on the south side of Zephyr Bay. As I said earlier, no one can get over there."

"Right you are, Leslie. My bad." Ned let out a chuckle.

Barbara groaned. "Ned and Leslie used to be an item," she said. "He lost his concentration."

"Seems like Mr. Wallace and everybody used to be an item," Ronnie said and immediately regretted it.

"Have you heard the latest rumor?" Barbara said.

"No. I'm sorta out of the loop for stuff like that."

"I think Ned and Carol Chapman are having a thing."

"No way." Ronnie's head popped up from behind the computer screen. "He's sleeping with the station manager's wife?"

"I'm telling you, kid. Ned is a force of nature."

"But I thought you and he were. . ."

Barbara shrugged. "We were. But you know what they say. Everything changes and everything ends. I guess technically, we still are, but I can tell it's about to end." She let out a wistful sigh.

On the TV screen, Leslie Lomax took command of the interview. "Ned. Here's by far the most important news for the survivors of Hurricane Atlas. They all need to hear this."

"Go ahead, Leslie. We're all ears."

"Ned, We're facing a situation out here that's not unlike what happened in New Orleans when Hurricane Katrina stuck."

"What's she talking about?" Barbara said.

"The canal," Ronnie said. "It has to be." He closed his laptop and joined Barbara in front of the TV monitor.

"You knew about this?" Barbara asked the intern.

"I keep up with the environmental stuff." Ronnie folded his arms across his chest. "Last year some of the developers in Bay St. Edwards pushed for the construction of a canal connecting Zephyr

Bay and the Gulf. It was supposed to shortcut the marshes and dry out more land for development. Expensive condos mostly. But if that area floods. . . well. . .You remember Katrina."

"Is that true?" Barbara said.

"As far as I know. It might not happen, but if the rain continues, the western end of the peninsula could wind up underwater."

On the screen, Leslie Lomax told her audience about the canal.

Ned looked like he had been slapped in the face. "Now, Leslie," he said in a patronizing tone. "I don't think we need the play the blame game here."

Leslie scowled into the camera. "I'm just reporting, Ned. And this is important news."

"It sounds more like conjecture to me," Ned said.

"The residents of Bay St. Edwards need to know that if the canals flood, cholera and dengue fever are a real possibility."

"If they don't drown first," Ronnie said. "More people die from inland flooding than any other hazard generated by hurricanes."

"Thanks for sharing," Barbara said.

"Tell Mr. Wallace to advise everyone to keep listening to a NOAA weather radio for further updates. They can get that information out a lot faster than we can."

"Good idea." Barbara relayed the message to Ned Wallace on the set.

"Let me remind everyone to keep your radio tuned to an NCAA weather channel for additional weather information."

Ronnie shook his head in disgust.

Suddenly, the TV monitor relaying the image of Leslie Lomax flickered and faded to black. The legend in the corner read "No Signal."

"Oh, no." Barbara looked frantically around the control room. "Where is Bert?" she said, referring to her tech man.

"He went to get sandwiches," Ronnie said. "He should be back any minute."

On the set, Ned looked confused.

"Stall," Barbara said into her mic. "We'll try to get Leslie back as quick as we can."

Ned looked puzzled.

"Tell them the difference in a hurricane and a tropical cyclone."

Ned smiled at the camera. "A lot of you have tweeted this question to the station. Why isn't Hurricane Atlas considered a tropical cyclone?"

"Who in the world would ask that?" Ronnie said, heading back to his computer.

"It's something Ned knows," Barbara said with a shrug.

"A tropical cyclone originates over tropical waters and has as closed surface wind circulation around a well-defined center."

Ronnie thought Ned sounded like he was reading from an encyclopedia.

Barbara's eyes swept the studio in search of her tech man.

"Hurricane Atlas on the other hand," Ned went on. "Is a hurricane where the winds exceed 74 miles per hour. But God knows the winds around here have been stronger than that. "We're getting reports of winds up to 160 miles per hour."

"Call Bert's cellphone," Barbara said. "We need to get him back here right now."

When Ronnie didn't respond, Barbara whirled around and opened her mouth to chastise him. But the expression on the intern's face pulled her up short. She followed his look of horror through the glass of the control booth, past Ned to the far edge of the set.

Jerry Chapman, the paunchy, graying station manager, stood quietly in the shadows watching Ned explain the difference between a tropical cyclone and a hurricane. Chapman's suit was soaking wet. His tie was pulled down and his thinning hair was plastered to his forehead. His mouth opened and closed like a fish.

In his right hand, he held an enormous automatic pistol.

CHAPTER 33

A COUPLE OF BLOCKS AWAY from the Manson of the Dead, Jackie and I sought refuge on the front porch of one of Dragon Hill's more modest houses. Probably only five or six bedrooms. We sat on the front porch and devoured the peanut butter, almonds and crackers, washing the feast down with the remains of the water bottle. No five-star gourmet meal ever tasted so good.

When we finished, I fished the smartphone out of my pocket. Jackie didn't ask where it came from.

I opened the phone and swiped upward. The screen asked for a password. In frustration I typed in 1234. That got me *invalid password*. Then an idea popped into my exhausted brain and I tried DUKE. The phone opened.

I punched in Skylar's number.

"Hel. . . Hello?" Skylar's voice sounded like she was at the bottom of a deep well.

"Skylar. It's your grandfather. I'm on my way. Tell me what's happening."

"Hello? Hello? I can't hear you. I can't hear anything but a buzzing sound. Please, whoever this is, we need help. My name is Skylar and my brother and I are trapped upstairs in the Emerald

Fields Mall. In a costume shop. The lower level is flooded and there are gross looking snakes in the water and dead people all over the concourse. The door to the shop won't open and we can't get out. Please help us."

"Hang on, darling. I'm coming as fast as I can. Skylar. Skylar!" I realized I was shouting as Skylar's voice broke up in a flurry of buzzing and static.

"We'll get there as fast as we can," Jackie said. "We'll be there in no time."

I looked up and managed a smile. "Then let's get going."

A block later, we both froze in the middle of the flooded street.

"I know that sound," I said. "I'd know it anywhere."

Jackie looked puzzled.

"It's a chopper," I said. "Hopefully with a rescue team on board." I spun around in the street until I spotted the helicopter hovering in the sky a hundred yards down the road. Jackie broke into a trot and I hobbled along behind her.

As we drew closer, I saw a red, white and blue NEWS logo on the side of the chopper and my heart sank. There was no rescue team.

Once we reached the top of the hill, we saw what had drawn the news people to Dragon Hill. A mansion had been reduced to rubble and a man and a woman were crawling over piles of brick and concrete and wood, pausing to bend over and shout each time they encountered an opening in the wreckage.

I dropped my backpack on the side of the road, put my hands on my knees and bent over to catch my breath.

Jackie stared at the people in the rubble. "What are they doing?"

"Looking for survivors," I said.

Jackie shook her head. "Of course."

Suddenly the man stood up and waved his arms at the chopper, his face contorted in rage. The woman joined him, waving frantically at the news people.

"If there are any survivors, that couple can't hear them because of the helicopter," Jackie said.

"That's my guess."

The copter dropped lower even though it was being buffeted by the wind. There was a cameraman in the passenger seat, aiming his camera like a gun at the exasperated man.

The man waved even harder, his exaggerated motions telling the chopper to leave. I could read his lips. "Go away! Go away!" He pointed to the rubble around him. He was in his late twenties, dressed in a golf shirt and a pair of gray shorts.

The woman saluted the chopper with her middle finger and went back to combing through the wreckage.

Seized by the sheer idiotic nature of the situation, I located a couple of baseball-sized rocks in the gravel shoulder of the road and chucked them at the helicopter.

I missed by a mile.

The pilot turned his head and Jackie and I waved our arms, signaling for the chopper to fly away. The pilot shot me the bird and I pegged a couple of more rocks his way. Jackie cupped her hand around her ear and pointed at the couple in the rubble. It was a more productive gesture than throwing rocks.

Whether the moron pilot figured out what he was doing or the cameraman got enough film, the helicopter tilted to the right and flew south toward the beach. The wind made the chopper lurch violently to the left. As the sound of the rotors faded into the distance, the ominous stillness of the post-storm world returned.

"What a bunch of idiots," I said. "They're crazy to have a helicopter out in this wind. Even the army or the National Guard won't try something that stupid."

"I hear you."

Jackie and I walked down the slope to the ruins. The young man in the golf shirt crawled over a pile of concrete to greet us. His face was covered in chalky dirt which made the whites of his eyes look large and out of proportion to his face. "The bastard wouldn't leave. It was obvious what we were doing. We couldn't hear anything. Someone could be trapped in there." He pointed to the rubble. "I live on the third floor of the house. I got out just in time."

"Nice going," I said.

"The woman over there lived on the floor below me. She and her sister. That's who we're looking for. You never know. Her sister could be trapped in there somewhere, crying for help."

"Josie! Josie! It's me," the woman shouted. "Josie, please answer me." She tore into a stack of bricks and started tossing them aside. "Josie, please."

Jackie and I exchanged pained looks.

"She's not going to make it much longer." The man indicated the woman frantically crawling over the rubble. "She's exhausted. I've tried to help her, but I'm afraid its hopeless. There's nobody alive in there."

I had to agree with him. Part of me said we should stay and help the woman look, but that seemed futile and Rand and Skylar were trapped in the mall and I desperately wanted to get going.

"Josie! Josie! It's me. Please." The woman's voice was a hoarse whisper, heavy with sadness and dread.

"Poor thing." Jackie said.

"A couple of army guys came by on ATVs a little while ago," the man said. "At least I think they were army. One of them had on camouflage but the other one wore a long black coat. I tried to wave them down, but they wouldn't even look at me." He shook his head in despair.

Shit, I thought. The ATVs again. The bastards that killed Mike in the bike shop. Then it hit me. The tracks outside the mansion. All-Terrain Vehicles. The dead guy with the severed hand. The hurricane was bad enough but this was insanity. Cold fear crept up my spine.

CHAPTER 34

THE CROMWELL MANSION WAS A showplace in Bay St. Edwards, rivaling anything built by Frank Lloyd Wright. The house was the pride and joy of Ian Cromwell, a young startup genius who had amassed a fortune by developing one of the first successful online dating sites and then selling it for untold millions.

Cromwell's palace had over 12,000 square feet, a ballroom, an indoor pool, an eight-car garage and more bedrooms than a small hotel. The young genius had bought all of the beachfront property across the road and to either side of the house to insure his privacy and provide him with an unobscured view of the majestic waters of the Gulf of Mexico.

Now, the Cromwell mansion had about 3,000 square feet, the far wing of the house having been carried away by Hurricane Atlas.

The violent storm had also left Susan Coffman trapped on the second floor of the palace. She vaguely remembered a blow to her head and there was blood on her face and on her blouse, but after the hurricane hit, everything seemed like a dream that she couldn't quite recall.

The house had been the pot of gold at the end of Susan's rainbow. Ian Cromwell had put the house on the market when he decided to move to L.A. and produce a movie starring his third wife. He had selected Susan to be his realtor. Seven percent of millions. Susan was beside herself.

She had found a potential buyer, a Chinese couple with grown children. The man owned a coast-to-coast string of women's apparel outlets and loved the mansion's view of the Gulf.

Susan had arrived late to show the house because of the trip to the zoo. The Chinese couple, unfortunately, valued punctuality. The woman was pissy when they started the tour of the residence. Then the storm picked up. Debris starting blowing everywhere and the sky turned gray and threatening. The man got nervous.

Susan adjusted her lucky bandana-scarf for the good karma it held and reassured the couple that she had checked the weather sites on her phone and there was nothing to worry about. It was a squall, nothing more. Then an uprooted palm tree blew past the front window and the couple fled. They drove away without making a commitment. Susan was crestfallen.

After the perspective buyers departed, Susan stayed behind, wandering from room to room, fantasizing what it would be like to be the lady of the manor of such a grand establishment.

She turned on the state-of-the-art sound system and danced through the house to a series of 80s hits from her childhood—Michael Jackson, Blondie, Duran, Duran. She felt like a princess in a castle, twirling beneath the 25-foot ceiling, lip-syncing in front of gold edged mirrors, dreaming of the prince who never seemed to show up.

But the sound of shattering glass and stucco being ripped from its mooring stopped her cold in mid-dance step.

A section of the east wing blew away and wind came howling into the living room, where Susan stood frozen. She was too frightened to move or even think.

The wind was accompanied by a wall of muddy debris-filled water that surged through the mansion, sweeping the Cromwell's elegant furniture in its wake.

The water knocked Susan over as she crossed the marble foyer, heading for the staircase that led to the second floor. She scrambled to her feet, slogged through the powerful current, grabbed her purse from the hall table and staggered to the stairs. She misjudged the first step and twisted her ankle, causing a sharp pain to rocket up her leg. By hopping on one foot and balancing herself on the bannister, she willed her way to the second-floor landing.

Two steps onto the landing and her ankle gave out. She toppled over, striking her head on the corner of a hall table. The world went dark for a moment then she collapsed on the floor and curled up into a tight ball, crying and screaming into the yowling wind that drowned out her cries for help. Tears slid down her cheeks and a tiny trickle of blood ran down her face from the wound to her head.

A minute later, another loud, ripping noise echoed through the Cromwell mansion as the bottom half of the staircase broke free, crashed into the foyer and washed away in the current. The top of the staircase dangled precariously over the water, creaking and moaning in the wind.

Susan crawled away from the stairwell and used a love seat on the landing to pull herself into a standing position. The pain in her ankle screamed in rebellion. She put her hand to her head and felt a golf ball sized lump growing next to her ear. Biting down hard on her lip, she hobbled into the master bedroom. One wall had been ripped away and a gaping hole looked out over the road and the furious waters of the Gulf beyond.

The storm blew debris past the hole in the bedroom wall, the wind howled and Susan sank to the floor. In a minute, her world went dark.

CHAPTER 35

"WHAT IS MR. CHAPMAN DOING with a gun?" Ronnie Crow stood next to Barbara in the window of the control booth of the TV station. They were transfixed, watching their station manager, who was lurking in the shadows of the news set, watching Ned Wallace while the weatherman broadcast a hurricane update.

Jane Palmer and Rakeem Hasan, the news anchors, sat frozen at the news anchor desk, their eyes darting back and forth between the camera and the gun-toting station manager. They kept their hands folded in front of them, smiles plastered on their faces.

Barbara's lips locked in a narrow line as the blood drained from her face.

"Damn," Ronnie said. "Mr. Chapman looks terrible. He doesn't even look like himself."

The station manager's normally well-coiffed sandy hair was plastered to his scalp. He needed a shave. His suit was rumpled and greasy. Ronnie could see Chapman's wide-open blood-shot eyes all the way across the set.

"My god. What kind of gun is that?" Ronnie said. "It's huge."

"It's a .50 caliber Desert Eagle semi-automatic." Barbara whispered. "It's one bad-ass pistol. Jerry's something of a gun nut."

"Oh." Ronnie swallowed.

"It looks like the worst of Atlas has moved to the northeast," Ned said, staring at the camera, oblivious of the gunman on his right.

"I think we're about to witness a workplace shooting," Barbara whispered through clinched teeth. She flipped down her mic. "Jane. You and Hasan get out of there now. Abandon the set. Right this minute. Move!"

The anchors stood, took off their microphones and did a fast walk away from the set.

"What's wrong with Mr. Chapman?" Ronnie said.

"Jerry's furious at Ned," Barbara said.

"Because of Ms. Chapman?"

"Not exactly."

"Then what on earth. . .?"

The station manager raised the gun, aimed it at Ned and lurched onto the news set.

"Shouldn't we shut down the broadcast?" Ronnie asked.

"No. Let it run. It's must see TV."

Ronnie stared at Barbara in disbelief. "That's cold," he said.

"That's TV," Barbara whispered. Then she spoke into her mic. "Galen. This is Barbara. Act natural. Keep the camera on Ned. Angle it as far away from Jerry as possible. But keep rolling. I think you're safe as long as you stay behind the camera."

The bearded cameraman looked up and the booth and nodded.

"The National Guard has issued a statement to the effect that. . ." Ned stopped in mid-sentence when he saw the gun leveled at him.

"EVERYTHING'S GONE." THE STATION MANAGER'S flat, even voice echoed through the boom mic into the control booth.

Ronnie realized he was holding his breath. He let it out slowly and quietly.

"The sonofabitch hurricane blew away my house," Chapman said. "Picked it up and blew it the hell away. Everything I own. Gone."

Ned took a step backward.

"The bastard picked up my car. My Jag. Picked it up like a little kid's toy. Smashed it into a Wendy's fast food place. Over on Ocean Drive. I loved that car. I saved for years to buy it. Now it's gone."

"Mr. Chapman," Ned said. "What, what. . . ." His eyes never left the gun. Words failed him.

"All I have left is my job. Running this pissant television station. I'm a middle manager. Big fuckin' deal."

Ned licked his lips. "Mr. Chapman. What. . . are you going to do? With that gun, I mean."

"I'm going to shoot you, you moron."

Ned frantically looked up at the booth, where Barbara and Ronnie stood next to each other, watching the unfolding drama on the set. Barbara held up her hands in a gesture of helplessness.

"When you're a kid," Chapman said. "You want to be a cowboy or a cop or a fireman. Not a middle manager. His voice remained calm.

When Ned made a move to walk away from the set, Chapman raised the pistol and, using both hands, aimed the gun at Ned's face.

"He seems to know how to use the gun," Ronnie whispered.

Barbara squeezed Ronnie's arm. "He does. He goes to the shooting range every week."

"This is the end of the line," Chapman said. "Middle manager at a little TV station in Crystal City, Florida. This is as high as it gets for me. Who woulda thought."

"Mr. Chapman," Ned said. "Listen to me. Atlas has got everybody spooked. I'm sorry about your car. I know that Jag meant the world to you."

"Shut up, you idiot."

Ned swallowed and wiped the sweat off his forehead with the back of his hand.

"Look at you, Wallace," Chapman said. "Every hair on your head in place. Your teeth are pearly white. Your voice sounds like it should come out of a radio. No wonder women find you irresistible. Look at me. I'm a fuckin' troll."

"No sir. That's not true."

Chapman sighted down the barrel of the Desert Eagle. "You're perfect for TV, Wallace. You're a fantasy. Like the covers of those romance novels. Hunky men. Yummy, yum. Let's face it. What you do, what we all do, is entertainment. We call what we do "news" but everybody knows it's entertainment. Right now, hundreds of people, at least the ones who still have a house, are watching us on their giant TV screens. Sitting safe and dry on their wraparound sofas, munching potato chips, waiting to see if the nutjob station manager is going to blow away the weather anchor on WBEC. How's that for entertainment?"

Barbara squeezed Ronnie's arm tighter. "Call 911," she whispered.

"We'll have to get in line," Ronnie whispered back. "All the emergency services are backed up, helping the survivors of the hurricane."

"Call anyway."

Ronnie nodded.

"That's all we all," Chapman rambled on. "An entertainment factory. Look at us." He gestured with the gun. "We're in the middle of a god-awful hurricane that's left hundreds of people homeless. Or dead for Christ's sake."

Ned's eyes stayed glued on the gun in Chapman's hand.

"And what are people doing? Watching TV. Grateful it wasn't them. Other people's misery is entertainment."

"Please put the gun away." Ned's normally steady voice cracked.

Chapman's stole a quick glance at the booth.

Ronnie cringed.

Chapman's voice went up a couple of octaves. "Hey, Suzie. Check it out. Some crazy guy just shot the local weatherman. Bring some more chips. And get me another beer."

Ned managed a weak smile.

Chapman shook his head. "Stay tuned, folks. We'll be right back to the dead weather guy right after these messages. "Hey people, if it's time to buy a new car, come on out to Dealin' Don's Discount Dodge Dealership, where the deals can't be beat anywhere on the Emerald Coast. And now, back to real people's ruined lives."

"Mr. Chapman, you really don't want to do this."

"Sure I do. I've got nothing left to lose. We've got hurricanes, mass shootings all right here on WBEC."

"Why are you doing this?"

"Okay, let's cut to the chase. I knew you were fucking my wife, Wallace. Knew it all along," Chapman said, sighting down the barrel of the pistol. "But, you know what? I didn't care. Not in the least. She's like you Wallace. A superficial moron. But you want to know why I really didn't give a rat's ass?"

Ned bit down on his lip.

"I didn't care because I was in love with Barbara."

CHAPTER 36

UP IN THE BOOTH, RONNIE turned to Barbara.

"He was obsessed," Barbara said. "Nothing ever happened."

Down on the set, Chapman licked his dry lips. "Barbara was smart and funny and sexy. I always knew we were destined to wind up together."

"Please, sir. Think about what you're doing." Ned's face was covered with a sheen of sweat.

"But it was like TV, Wallace," Chapman said. "It was fantasy. Just when Barbara and I were getting close, she fell in love with you. Head over heels. You were all she could talk about. Do you know how hard that was for me? To hear the woman I love blabbering about an idiot like you."

"I. . . didn't mean for it to happen," Ned said.

"It hurt, Wallace. Hurt real bad."

Ronnie sucked in air through his nose. "Miss Stanhope," he said. "You've got to go out there and talk to Mr. Chapman. He has strong feelings for you. He'll listen to you. You could get him to put down the gun."

Barbara arched her eyebrows. "Are you nuts? Look at him. Look at those eyes. Did you hear what he said? A mass shooting.

As in more than one person. He's not just planning to kill Ned. He's going to kill me next. You're the one who's got to go out there. There's no one else. Just stall him. The cops will be here in a minute."

"I don't think so," Ronnie said. "I got a busy signal when I called 911."

"Then talk him into putting away the gun."

"Miss Stanhope, I don't think I'm the one to. . . "

"You're the only one. He doesn't know you. You haven't hurt him. He doesn't have any reason to kill you. You can talk to him. Come on, Ron. The ball's in your court."

Refusing Barbara Stanhope was not an option for Ronnie Crowe. She was the most beautiful woman he had ever seen. Looking like a sniveling worm in front of her was out of the question. His princess was asking him to slay the dragon.

Barbara handed him a small ear piece so she could talk to him on the news set and Ronnie slipped out of the booth and down the stairs. He stopped outside the arc of lights. His heart raced and his palms were drenched. He had never done anything remotely brave in his young life. Now he was about to confront a crazed gunman. He looked over his shoulder at the exit door. Bolting and running was a possibility. FEAR stood for Fuck Everything and Run.

Chapman swung the gun around and aimed it at Ronnie. "Who the hell are you?"

Ronnie's throat tightened. "I'm, uh. Ronnie Crow," he croaked. "Miss Stanhope's intern."

"Are you banging her too?"

"Who me? No. No sir. Not me."

"Get the hell out of here, kid. I got no beef with you. Go on, get lost."

"Mr. Chapman, listen." Ronnie struggled to make his voice sound normal. "Hurricane Atlas has affected all of us." Despite his best efforts, his voice squeaked. "The storm has ruined our perspectives, turned our whole world upside down. It's destroyed our ability to think straight."

"Are you kidding me?" Chapman said. "Ruined our perspective? I've lost everything, kid. Everything that matters. Gone. My house, my Jag, my wife, Barbara. Yeah. You might say my perspective is ruined. Hell, you might say Atlas has torn away all pretext of life as we know it. So, here's the perspective that's changed as far as I'm concerned. I don't care anymore. If I shoot Ned here. If I shoot Barbara. Hell, if I shoot you. None of it matters anymore. The only people who care are those bozos watching us out there on their TV screens and they're all thinking, 'why doesn't he hurry up and pull the trigger so I can go make a sandwich.'"

Desperation seized Ronnie's gut. What do you say to someone who is unhinged and has a gun? As far as Jerry Chapman was concerned, his life was gone and it wasn't coming back.

"Okay, Mr. Chapman. I hear you." Ronnie opted for a shot in the dark. "But I think we can still do some good here. All of us at WBEC. It's not too late. People are desperate for information. As long as we're on the air and they have a generator, we can give them that information. People are searching for their loved ones, or trying to find shelters, or finding out what's happened in other communities on the Emerald Coast. We can provide a needed service. But not if. . .you know. . . if you. . ."

Chapman looked at Ronnie like the intern was babbling in a foreign tongue. But he lowered the gun.

Ronnie thought he was making headway. "Those trapped on the Bay St. Edwards peninsula—they need us. You and me and Ms. Stanhope and Mr. Wallace."

The station manager swung the gun back on Ned, who let out a low moan.

Barbara crossed her arms over her chest and whispered into her mic. "You're doing great. Keep it up. He might buy it. He's a bit of an idealist. Keep it up, Ronnie."

Ronnie kept it up. "The survivors in Bay St. Edwards need to know if help is on the way. They need tips on how to survive until that help gets there. We can give them those tips. Maybe even save someone's life."

Chapman looked confused.

"Let me have the gun, sir," Ronnie said. "You can go down to your office and lay down on the sofa and rest. You've been through hell. You need to shut your eyes for a while. How does that sound? We can find some people who can help you. Then we can go on helping all the survivors out there. Come on, Mr. Chapman. What'd you say? You don't really want to kill anybody. Too many people have already died today."

Chapman licked his lips. His gun hand began to tremble.

Ned's legs buckled and he leaned against the anchor desk. Sweat dripped off the tip of his nose.

Barbara switched frequencies and spoke into her mic. "Ned. Listen to me. Pull yourself together. I know Jerry and what Ronnie is telling him is working. You've got to help Ronnie seal the deal. Touch your tie if you can hear me."

Ned managed a lopsided smile. His hand went to the knot of his tie.

"Now look straight into the camera and say exactly what I tell you."

Ned adjusted his tie, took a deep breath and smiled at the camera. "Here's the latest update on the aftermath of Hurricane Atlas. The governor has declared the Emerald Coast a disaster area and emergency teams from FEMA and the state police are their way to the area."

Chapman looked at the weatherman and raised and lowered his gun in a fit of indecision.

"The National Guard has issued a statement that they are going to attempt to land helicopters on the Bay St. Edwards Peninsula as soon as possible." Ned's voice gained confidence as he went along. "This is good news for the survivors in that area. Hang on, folks. The cavalry is on the way."

Chapman glared at Ned.

Ronnie inched closer to the station manager. "Please, sir," he said in a low voice. "Let me have the gun. I know you've suffered terrible losses and you feel angry and frustrated. But you won't always feel this way. You've survived the worst storm in American history. If you made it through that, you can survive anything."

"Barbara. . . my house. . . my car. . . all gone." Tears slide down the station manager's cheeks. His lower lip trembled out of control.

"You need to rest, Mr. Chapman," Ronnie said. "Let me have the gun. We can go down to your office and you can lay down for a while. What'd you say?"

Chapman looked at Ronnie like he was seeing the intern for the first time. He shook his head. "You're a good kid. You're right about what we do here. I don't know what I was thinking. We do offer hope and we certainly offer information. It's good work. It's important."

"It sure is."

Chapman thrust the gun at Ronnie with a trembling hand. "I'm going to promote you, kid. Give you a raise. The whole works."

"Thank you, sir." Ronnie took the gun and held it away from him like it was about to explode. "The hurricane has changed all of us," he said. "Come on, let's go get that rest."

Chapman's nodded. His shoulder's slumped.

Ronnie put the gun on the news anchor desk and guided Chapman off the set and down the hallway to the administrative offices. As they slowly made their way down the hall, Ronnie could hear Ned's broadcast voice behind him.

"Even though the center of the hurricane has passed, we can still expect heavy rains and cloud cover for the next few days. Then we can start the rebuilding process in Crystal City and Bay St. Edwards and the entire Emerald Coast area."

CHAPTER 37

AFTER SUSAN WOKE UP, SHE cowered in the corner of the bedroom, covering her head with her arms, shrieking and sobbing as the wind slammed debris into the Cromwell mansion and the rain gushed into the room through the giant hole that had once been a wall.

Half an hour later, the storm subsided.

Susan's clothes were soaking wet and her ankle was swollen and had turned a nasty shade of purple. A slow and painful trip to the second story landing revealed that the staircase was gone along with two thirds of the mansion, leaving her trapped on the second floor.

She hobbled back into the bedroom, mumbling positive mantras to herself. "Winners never quit. Always be moving forward." They didn't help. There was no way around it. She was in a dire situation.

She pulled her phone out of her purse and punched in her dad's number.

Come and get me, Daddy. I'm in bad trouble. I need you. I need you to throw your arms around me and tell me everything is going to be alright.

The phone was dead.

She tried Skylar and Rand with the same lack of results and panic washed over her.

Susan limped into the owner's suite bathroom and checked the contents of the medicine cabinet. Viagra didn't seem to be of much use.

Back in the bedroom, she braced herself on the side of the giant hole and called for help. But the thought dawned on her that there were no neighboring houses and hence, no neighbors. A soul shattering sense of aloneness swept over her.

Negative thoughts attacked from all sides like an invading army—she would starve to death, dehydration would set in, another storm would hit and carry away the rest of the Cromwell mansion with Susan in it. She summoned the wisdom of the hundreds of positive thinking books she had read and every motivational tape she had ever listened to. It was time to awaken the giant within and get on the energy bus.

But the giant was sleeping soundly and the energy bus was out of gas. Exhausted from the struggle, Susan burst into tears.

Smells from outside wafted into the bedroom—fish, sewage, citrus. Across the road, the waters of the Gulf churned with white foam and ominous gray clouds hovered close to the earth.

She sank to her knees. The music from downstairs forced its way into the bedroom. The sound system from downstairs was still pumping out the greatest hits of the 1980s—"*Hungary Like the Wolf; Girls Just Want to Have Fun.* The house apparently came with an automatic back-up generator and the joyous techno-pop sounds of her youth mocked Susan in her agony. Now the songs sounded like the soundtrack from hell.

The music took her back to her childhood—the raucous parties she never went to, the football players who never ask her out. She wished she could have those years back. Not study so much. Not be so driven. Her dad had begged her to lighten up and enjoy her teen years. But what did he know? He was an ex-jock high school teacher who was going nowhere. Not Susan. She had big plans. Big ambitions.

Now she realized she should have listened to her father. I mean, he really wasn't such a bad guy. One time, when her car had stalled out on a lonely mountain road, her dad had left a dinner party and picked her up. If only he could come and pick her up now.

Suddenly Susan heard a distant and muffled sound. The cellphone in her purse. She ripped open the purse, grabbed the phone and held it to her ear. "Hello. Skylar? Rand? Dad? Hello. Hello. The silence on the other end was like a slap in the face. "Hello. Hello." The silence grew louder.

She looked back into her purse and the sight of her .38 Smith and Wesson comforted her. Big Brother wanted to take away her gun but she and her NRA allies had fought Big Brother at every turn. And now her efforts had been rewarded. She rested her hand on the cold metal and relaxed. No matter what horrors came her way, she would be in charge.

Control was the cornerstone of Susan's life. She regarded herself as a rugged individualist, who made her own way in the world. Poor people were poor because they were too stupid to be rich. Susan planned on being rich. As long as she could maintain control.

The phone went off again. This time Skylar's picture appeared on the screen. It was a photograph from her last birthday when she wore a straw fedora at a jaunty angle, while she mugged for the camera.

"Skylar. Are you alright?"

"Mommy, help."

The connection was full of crackling static and strange beeping sounds. Susan shouted into the phone. "Oh, thank God. Where are you, sweetie?"

"We're in the mall but we can't get out. I called Bugs and tried to tell him but we got cut off."

"Calm down. Everything is going to be okay."

"No it's not." Skylar's sobbing grew louder.

Susan bit down on her lower lip.

"Can you see anyone else?"

"Not from here. Everybody ran when part of the roof ripped off. All this water rushed in and Rand and I ran up the escalator to the second floor. Then we ran into this creepy Halloween store. Now the whole first floor of the mall is under all this yucky water. Come and get us, Mommy."

Susan swallowed hard, passed the lump in her throat. "It'll be a while before I can get there," she said, surveying the bedroom of the Cromwell mansion and the water of the Gulf across the road. "But don't worry. I'll be there."

"Bugs is coming," Skylar said.

"What?"

"I talked to Bugs. Kinda. The phone was all messed up and I told him we were in the mall and he said he was coming to get us."

Susan sighed. The chances of her father making it to the mall from wherever he was were remote at best. Old age had knocked him down for the count and he wasn't in any shape to save the kids from the mall.

"That's great, sweetie. I'm sure he'll be there in a little while. How's your brother?"

"He banged his head really hard when one of the windows in the store blew out. But we found all these t-shirts and stopped the bleeding. But he's all pale and funny looking. And he can barely talk."

"Let me talk to him."

"Just a sec."

"M. . . Mo. . . Mom?"

"It's okay, baby. I'll be there as soon as I can. I promise."

Rand mumbled something that sounded like "mimfub."

Her son was in shock. Maybe he had a concussion. Susan sucked in frantic gulps of air through her nose. The phone went silent. "Rand! Rand! Can you hear me? Rand." Nothing but silence.

Panic and frustration overcame Susan. She hobbled around the exposed bedroom, frantically searching for a way out of her prison. She was too high up to jump to the ground and there was no one around to help her. She had to get to her children, but there was no way out.

A strange sound brought her head up.

On the road below, she watched a wall of rock, mud and debris push its way westward. The drains were overwhelmed and couldn't handle the excess water. The landscape quickly became unrecognizable. Everything was under water.

Susan's thirst became acute. Her lips were parched and her throat constricted. She couldn't remember the last time she ate. She knew she had to act, but meaningful action seemed impossible. She put her back against the wall and slid down into a sitting position, resting her arms on her knees.

Outside, the wind picked up but Susan barely noticed. She rested her back against the wall, too exhausted to sleep or cry. The pulsating sounds of the 80s—*Karma Chameleon*, *Billie Jean*—grew far away as she drifted into a fear-induced trance.

CHAPTER 38

SUSAN WOKE UP TO THE echo of voices. They sounded far away, but they were real. She struggled to her feet, but the first step on her puffy ankle sent waves of pain up her leg. Hopping on one foot, she made it to the craggy hole that looked out over the road and the Gulf beyond.

She scanned the horizon. The Gulf waters were still choppy and the waves lapped at the beach with promises of devastation still to come.

Then on the right side of the flooded road, Susan saw a man and a woman walking on the shoulder on the Gulf side. The going was slow, the terrain torturous, but the couple kept slogging. The man was a middle-aged African-American, dressed in a gray suit with a pink dress shirt. His tie was pulled down and hung loosely at his throat. He was soaking wet.

The woman was younger. Her dark blond hair was pulled back in a tight knot. She wore a green jacket and a pair of blue sweatpants and a neon running shoe on her right foot. Her left foot was covered with nothing but a dirty white sock. The lack of a shoe caused her to limp.

Susan's hopes soared.

"Help! Help! Up here!" She waved her arms. "Help! I'm trapped up here."

The couple didn't look up.

"Please help! Up here!" Susan moved to the center of the opening and waved both arms.

The couple trudged on with their heads down, hunched against the wind.

Susan hobbled into the bathroom and retrieved a white bath towel. By the time she got back to the hole, the couple had almost reached the mansion. She waved the towel. "Please! Look up here! I need help!"

The couple lowered their heads against the wind.

The horror of the situation engulfed Susan. The wind and the crashing of the waves drowned out her cries. The couple wasn't going to look up. They were going to keep walking down the road, past the shell of the Cromwell mansion and then disappear.

One last scream for help rode away on the howling wind.

The bath towel slipped to the floor. "Please help me." Susan's voice dropped to a whisper. *Daddy, please come and get me.*

The couple passed the mansion.

Suddenly the woman stopped. She and her companion turned around and looked back down the road. Susan followed their glance.

A pair of ATVs roared down the flooded road, pushing water high in the air in their wake. One of the riders had on an army field jacket and a soft brimmed military field hat. The other rider was a blond young man with a dark streak at his temple. His long black coat billowed behind him. They both wore sunglasses despite the heavy haze that hung over the landscape.

Susan's hopes swelled again.

She seized the towel off the floor and waved it back and forth. "Up here! Hey! Look up here! Help!" But the combination of the wind and the waves and the roar of the ATV engines drowned out her pleas.

The ATVs came to a halt in front of the couple on the road. The four figures huddled in front of a pair of tall dunes. The man in the dark coat appeared to ask a question and the woman began talking non-stop, gesturing with her hands, pointing down the road. Her companion nodded in agreement. The ATV riders seemed to be asking for directions.

Every time any of the group raised their head, Susan frantically waved her towel. To no avail.

The blond soldier shrugged and shook his head. His buddy nodded and restarted his ATV. The man in the suit shook his head. The other rider started his own vehicle.

The man in the suit lunged forward and grabbed the soldier's arm. He was begging. The rider shoved him away and turned his ATV toward the road.

Susan watched in disbelief as the man in the suit staggered backward and then lunged forward, grabbling the rider by the lapels.

Susan dropped the towel. Her hands went to her mouth as she watched the rider shove the man away. Before the man could recover, the rider in the field hat gave his ATV full throttle and plowed into the man in the suit, knocking him backwards into the dunes.

"Oh, my god," Susan said out loud.

The young woman whirled and sprinted toward the beach away from the riders, but the lack of a shoe hindered her progress.

The rider with the dark streak in his hair produced a shotgun and balanced the stock against his thigh and shot the fleeing girl in the back. A series of dark red splotches appeared on her jacket as she lurched forward and fell on the wet sand.

The man in the gray suit struggled to his knees and then collapsed on the side of the road.

Susan emitted a series of guttural moans and sank to her knees.

Black Streak pulled his ATV next to his partner and pointed down the road to the east and then, as Susan watched in disbelief, the other rider pointed to the shell of the Cromwell mansion.

Moments earlier, Susan had done everything in her power to make herself visible to the people on the road. Now she lay down on her side and froze, desperate to remain as motionless as possible, hidden from the sadistic killers. Her teeth chattered as waves of fear racked her body.

Black Streak nodded his agreement. He tossed his shotgun onto the sandy beach, gesturing to his partner that he was out of ammunition. The other rider shrugged. They throttled their engines and the two ATVs executed U-turns in the middle of the flooded road, crossed the highway and headed straight for the Cromwell mansion.

CHAPTER 39

"LOOK OVER THERE." JACKIE STOPPED and pointed. "It's the top of the hotel. The one that's across the street from the Emerald Fields Mall."

I looked where she was pointing. Through my cataract haze I could make out a white structure above the treetops in the distance. It could have been a hotel or it could have been a space ship from Mars.

We had run out of water a long time ago and my mouth was a desert. I felt woozy and hoped dehydration wasn't closing in on me. My lips had cracked and were starting to peel.

Buoyed by the sight of our destination, we picked up our pace. The floodwater had gotten so deep on the road, we found it impossible to do anything except take measured steps through the ankle-deep muck that filled the crown of the road so we fell back into the slow, steady rhythm of our march to the mall.

We turned northward, away from the Gulf, but the salty smell of the ocean clung to the air. I had given up my vigilant search for snakes and alligators. What will be will be.

Jackie stopped beside a small ditch where some blackish rainwater had accumulated. “Maybe it wouldn’t hurt if we just rinsed our mouths and spit out the water. I’m so damn thirsty.”

I looked at the water. It was a tempting offer, but I knew better. “We can’t do it,” I said. “That’s how you get cholera and a bunch of other diseases. It’s not worth the risk. Trust me. I’m sure we can find some bottled water at the mall. Just hang on a little longer.”

Jackie’s face fell. “I know you’re right,” she şaid. “Discipline has never been my strong suit.”

“Try not to think about it. I know that’s a tall order. But we gotta keep going.”

“Thanks,” Jackie said with a sigh. “You just saved me.”

“We’re saving each othcr,” I said as we resumed walking. “I couldn’t have done this without you.”

Jackie smiled. “You would have made it,” she said. “You’re driven by love and you’re a determined man. You’re resourceful as hell and your grandchildren are lucky to have you in their lives. So is your daughter. She just doesn’t know it yet. I know you love her and I know you’re worried sick about what might have happened to her. But let’s get the kids first and then we’ll find Susan. Agreed?”

“Agreed,” I said.

We slogged on, our steps involuntarily getting slower and slower. “How about you?” I asked. “You got family around here?”

A cloud moved across Jackie’s face. “No. Not around here. Not any place.”

I knew better than to push the matter.

Jackie was a mystery. She was a beautiful, intelligent woman but a part of her was sealed off. I was curious because I was genuinely fond of her.

"The flooding is getting worse," Jackie said, changing the subject. "If the canals have flooded we're going to be deep in the dog's business."

"What was it Dorothy Parker said?" I indicated the flooded street. "What fresh new hell is this?"

Jackie laughed despite the severity of the situation. I suspected she had faced adversity before. She had that kind of steel about her.

"We'll just have to do what we have to do," I said.

Jackie grinned. "Where's that grumpy old geezer I started out with?"

Being around Jackie made me feel like a guy rather than an old guy. She never adopted that condescending tone so many people take with older men and women. "When the going gets tough, the tough get going," I said. "My old football coach use to say that at least ten times at every practice."

"Sounds like words to live by," Jackie said.

We laughed again. "Our whole world has changed," I said. "The world we knew before is long gone."

"Maybe we have to lose everything before we can start over."

What Jackie said was a cliché but she said it with such conviction I wondered if she might be right.

"You know what I think I'm going to do after we get your grandkids and this nightmare is over?" Jackie said.

"What?"

"Go to community college."

"No kidding."

"No kidding. I always wanted to go to college. When I was a little girl I loved to read. Still do."

"What kind of stuff do you read?"

"Mysteries, mostly. I've read Sue Grafton A to Y. Janet Evanovich. I love the Jack Reacher books. You're kinda like Reacher. Tall. Resourceful. You know your stuff. Only you're more mature."

"I'll take that as a compliment."

"You should."

"You like books?"

"Absolutely. I read a lot of history. There's some good stuff out there. Candice Millard is terrific. So is Michael Korda. They really know how to make history come to life."

"When we get out of this mess, maybe you could tell me about some of those books. I'd like to read more thoughtful stuff, but I don't know where to start."

"It would be my pleasure. Once a teacher, always a teacher."

"There's so much I want to learn," Jackie said. "I mean there's so much I don't know. Maybe Atlas has freed me to do that. I want to do it before I get too old."

I looked at Jackie with admiration. "You've got a long way to go on that count."

"Back at you, John. You hear me? Not too old."

"Message received."

The top of the hotel disappeared from view as we slogged on through the muddy flood water. We were heading in the right direction and any minute we would stumble into a clearing and there would be the Emerald Fields Mall. Then Jackie and I would find Skylar and Rand and the story would have a happy ending.

We followed the winding, flooded road on and on. Up hills and past houses and gas stations that had been crushed by the hurricane. The landscape of despair. But no mall.

"Okay," Jackie said. "Since you're such a decrepit old geezer, why don't we take five and sit down on that rise over there. You need to rest those creaky old bones."

I grinned. Jackie needed to rest.

"Yeah. You're right. I could use a break."

"Just a few minutes," Jackie said. "I'm bushed." Her face was bathed in sweat and her shirt clung to her body. Her hair hung in damp strings around her face.

"That's the problem with you young folks," I said. "No stamina. You've all gone soft. Back in my day, we walked five miles to school and ten miles back."

"Barefoot in the snow. Yeah. Yeah." Jackie gave me a friendly punch on the arm.

We collapsed on the damp grass in front of an oak tree that had been stripped of its leaves. "God, what I wouldn't give for a glass of wine, a hot shower and a long nap."

"Hold that thought," I said. "Until we get out of here."

Jackie sighed. "Do you think we will? Get out of here. Get out of this nightmare."

"I couldn't keep going if I didn't think so," I said.

Jackie put her hand on my shoulder. "Look who's spouting optimism now."

"Even us old guys see the sunshine every once in a while."

"But the flooding is getting worse."

"I've noticed."

"If this wind doesn't die down, they're never going to be able to land helicopters on the peninsula. We're trapped."

"You're stealing my lines," I said, with as much levity as I could manage.

"You're all right," Jackie said.

I did a mock bow. "Maybe you're right," I said. "Maybe we're in a new world and all the rules are gone. No future. No past. Nothing but right now."

"Could be the start of something wonderful. You never know."

I looked into Jackie's green eyes. The start of something wonderful. That had a ring to it. Who knew what could happen in a new world.

CHAPTER 40

THE ATVS ROARED TO A stop in front of the Cromwell mansion.

Upstairs, Susan lay frozen in a fetal position in front of the hole that used to be the bedroom wall. She could see the two young men below and silently prayed that they wouldn't look up and see her in the jagged opening.

They weren't soldiers. That was for sure. One of them wore a camouflage jacket and a field hat, but his blond hair poured over his collar. The other one had a black streak in his hair and wore a long back coat. They were identical twins.

Susan couldn't hear them over the roar of the ATV engines and the yowling of the wind, but it was clear they were coming into the house. She had to pee, but there was no way that was going to happen. She forced her body to remain still. If the twins saw her, they would kill her like they had killed the couple across the road.

The twins cut the engines of their vehicles and disappeared under the portico. The front door had been ripped away by the hurricane and Susan could hear their voices in the downstairs foyer.

She scrambled to her feet and started toward the bedroom door, which she had left wide open. The first step on her swollen ankle sent a stabbing pain up to her knee. She let out an involuntary cry and covered her mouth with her hand. She hobbled the rest of the way across the room and pulled the door closed. She didn't close it all the way for fear the twins would hear it click shut.

Angry voices carried from the foyer, rising above the greatest hits of the 80s.

"Stupid bastard. I ask him how far it was to the mall and all he wanted to do was yak about his house getting trashed in the storm. Like I give a shit."

"You showed him."

"Damn straight. I ask a man a question, I deserve an answer. Not of bunch of pitiful crap about his house and his missing wife. I don't give a rat's ass."

"Me either. All I want to do is get to the Drug Rite. I'm starting to flame out."

"Pop another Viking."

"I'm all out. That's what I'm telling you. It's getting serious. All I can think about are big jars of Oxy in the back of the Drug Rite. Where is the stupid mall? I know it wasn't this far south when we were here before. Goddamn hurricane rearranged the whole peninsula."

Susan heard a series of crashes echoing through the foyer.

"Whoa. Calm down, bro. The mall can't be too far from here."

Susan's mind raced out of control. The mall. The Drug Rite. Skylar and Rand. Oh, God, no.

"There's bound to be some stuff here. Rich people like us keep doctors on the payroll. They get all the stuff they want. Perks and Viks and Vals Come on. Let's search the bathrooms. Then we'll head for the mall."

"Okay. But we gotta hurry, bro. I'm really starting to hurt."

"Won't take a second."

Susan held her breath and listened to the banging and thumping from downstairs.

"Whoa. Dude. Check this out. Look what I found in the drawer in this stupid little table. I mean, look at this."

"You found a gun? Awesome."

"Not just a gun, my man. A Glock 19 9mm Lugar. Holds fifteen rounds."

"But. . ."

"Right here in the same drawer. A whole box of ammo. Nobody's gonna mess with us now. I mean nobody. We're the fuckin' Kings of the Peninsula."

"You got that right. Now let's find some drugs and get the hell out of here."

Susan's body convulsed in fear. These men were beyond crazy. They were homicidal. There was no telling what they might do. She heard the sound of footsteps running through the foyer, followed by doors slamming. Angry shouts rang through the mansion.

"Nothing! Nothing in this bathroom."

"Nothing in the back bedrooms either. Aspirin. First aid cream. Who the hell lives here? What kind of people don't keep prescription drugs in the medicine cabinet?"

"Let's try upstairs."

"Think again, bro. Check out the staircase. The sonofabitch collapsed."

"Damn."

"No way we're gonna get up there."

"I bet that's where they keep the good stuff. Up where the grown-ups live. Shit. There's got to be a way to get up there."

"Forget it."

"Come on dude, how can we get up there?"

Panic seized Susan. The twins were coming upstairs. Somehow. Some way. They were going to get upstairs and kill her like they had killed the woman by the dunes. Rape and kill her.

They were insane. Crazy killers turned loose by the hurricane. After they killed her, they were going to the mall. Going to the Drug Rite to loot the pharmacy.

She had to stop them.

Susan crawled back across the bedroom floor and grabbed her purse off the table. She ripped open her bag and whipped out her gun. The pointy headed liberal fools wanted to take away her gun, but the .38 was the only thing that stood between Susan and the crazed barbarian hordes.

She hefted the gun in her hand. The weight of the metal immediately calmed her down. She was in control. When the twins came through the bedroom door on their insane drug hunt she would blow them into oblivion.

Holding the gun in one hand, she dug back into her purse. Into the little zipper pocket where she kept the bullets for the .38. Her gun safety instructor had told her again and again that it was folly to keep a loaded gun in her purse with kids in the house. So she hid her bullets in the pocket in the back of the purse.

Only the pocket was empty.

There were no bullets.

Susan let out a gasp. Oh, God, no, no. Please. I couldn't be that stupid. Then she remembered. She had been running late to her appointment at the Cromwell mansion. As usual, her father drove too slowly. Pokey, pokey, pokey. His driving made her late. Then Rand needed something. He was so needy. That made her even later. She had to change purses from the casual purse she had taken to the zoo to the more formal one she used when she interacted with clients.

She had stood at the hall table in her house and dumped her lipstick, her compact, a bottle of Advil, her wallet, her cellphone and her gun into the purse. Everything except the bullets.

Now she was going to die for her stupid mistake.

She heard a loud pounding noise from the foyer below. They were coming. Somehow, they were coming. Coming to kill her.

Susan hobbled to a chair and turned it where it faced the door. She collapsed into the chair and aimed her empty gun at the doorway. The wait was agonizing. Her sweat-drenched blouse clung to her back. Her ankle throbbed. Her gun hand trembled. She waited. And waited.

"FUCK THIS. IT'S NOT GONNA work." The voice carried upstairs from the foyer. "We can't get up there, man. There's just no way. The rest of those stairs are gonna go any minute."

"Chill, dude."

"Chill this. I gotta get some stuff. Like yesterday. I don't care what's up there. Screw it. Let's head for the mall."

"Whoa, bro. Don't go junkie on me."

"Junkies in the apocalypse! That's what we are. Come on man. There's all the stuff we want at the drug store. It's a drug store. A store full of drugs. Come on. We're never gonna get upstairs."

A long silence followed. "Okay. You win. Screw it. There probably isn't any stuff up there anyway. Let's boogie."

"Now you're talking."

Susan heard more banging from the foyer. "Hurry up! Don't worry about that. Let's just go."

"Yeah, yeah. I'm right behind you. It's done. Let's go."

More noise. Then Susan heard the roar of the ATV engines in front of the house. She let out a long sigh of relief.

Then she smelled the smoke.

CHAPTER 41

THE ROAD WAS NOTHING MORE than a dirt trail. The foliage on either side had been swept away by the hurricane and the resulting landscape looked like the dark side of the moon.

My anxiety over getting to the mall and finding Rand and Skylar felt like physical pain. I did a three sixty and took stock of our possibilities. "Normally," I said. "The sun will help you out. It always rises in the east and sets in the west. But I can't even find the sun in this haze. Moss grows on the north side of trees, but I don't see any trees."

"Me either."

I let out a long sigh. I had about reached the outer limits of my ability to tolerate frustration.

"That leaves us with dealer's choice," Jackie said. "What'd you think?"

I looked up and down the road. "Let's go left," I said. "But that's just a hunch."

"A hunch is all we got. It'll have to do."

I shifted my backpack to a more comfortable position on my shoulder.

After about a mile, we came around a sharp bend in the road and encountered the site of what had once been an RV park.

Some of the giant vehicles had been crushed by the hurricane, while others had been picked up and tossed round. Their concrete pads sat empty in the fields to our right. Some of the RVs had landed on top of cars and glass and metal littered the field and the road. Ragged dolls and stuffed animals lay scattered in the mud.

"Look," Jackie said, not trying to hide her excitement. "Over there. It's an asphalt road. It intersects with this cow path we've been on. I bet that road will take us back to familiar territory."

I grinned. "What are we waiting for?"

The asphalt road was under an inch of water, but the going was a lot easier than it had been on the dirt trail. We had to be getting close to the Emerald Fields Mall.

"How are you holding up?" Jackie asked after a while. "Your limp seems worse."

"It's okay," I said. "A couple of days ago, it was all I could do to get back and forth to the refrigerator for a beer. But now? We've covered a lot of territory and I'm still going. I'm the Geriatric Energizer Bunny."

Jackie laughed. "Listen, old man. You're putting me to shame. I may have a few years on you, but you're one tough dude."

"I love those kids," I said. "They need our help and I'm not going to let them down. Hip or no hip. Pain or no pain."

"I like the sound of that," Jackie said. "Our help. I'm afraid helping people hasn't been something I've spent much time doing."

"What did you do before the hurricane hit? Before all of this?" I gestured at the bleak landscape.

Jackie pursed her lips and thought for a minute. "I was a stripper," she said, looking straight ahead at the road. "At a little dive out on the highway to Crystal City."

There was a time in my life when that revelation would have resulted in a harsh judgment on my part. But that time had come and gone. We were in the middle of a live nightmare and Jackie had helped me out of a couple of tight spots. She had kept my spirits up and stuck with me when the going got tough. That was all I needed. I didn't give a damn what she did before I met her.

"I've never been to college," Jackie said. "I didn't have any marketable skills. I needed money. What else can I say?"

"You don't need to say anything," I said. "We all do what we have to do. It's called life."

"I was just a stripper," Jackie said. "I didn't go the extra mile. Not one time."

"Hey. None of my business."

"I was a stripper, not a whore. There's a big difference."

"You don't owe me. . ."

"Half of it's the costume," Jackie kept her eyes on the road. "I was a school girl for a while. Then a cop with handcuffs. Then a cowgirl. Guys love that stuff."

I didn't know what to say.

"I took off my clothes, gave the guys an eyeful. Gave 'em a thrill. They gave me some cash. It wasn't neurosurgery. It beat working fast food or working on an assembly line back in Ohio."

"It's okay by me," I said. "You don't have to explain a thing."

We walked on in silence for a while, our feet sloshing through the muddy floodwater.

"I'm glad you told me that," I said as we rounded a bend in the road.

"Yeah?"

"Yeah. It makes it easier for me to tell you something."

Jackie knitted her eyebrows. "Like what?"

"Like why I can never go back to Colorado. If I ever try to go back, they'll throw me in jail so fast it would make your head spin. I'm banned from the state forever."

"Ouch."

"You can say that again. I did a stupid thing and let my temper get the best of me. When you do stupid things, there are consequences."

"So I've heard."

I took a deep breath. I had never spoken to anyone, not even Susan, about my exile from Colorado. Now seemed like the time.

"My wife got the hots for another man," I said. "Personally, I think she got the hots for his money, but I guess I'll never know for sure."

"It happens," Jackie said.

"Yeah, it does. The clown was the chairman of the board of the school where I taught. Inherited money, real estate, banks, you name it. Guy's name was Owen Baldwin. He was ten years younger than me. President and CEO of Tech World International. A scratch golfer."

A warm breeze swept paper cups and fast food wrappers across the road.

"They met at one of our high school basketball games. My wife told me it was love at first sight. I wanted to puke. The truth was my wife was sick and tired of hearing about my hip and how I couldn't hike or ski or play handball anymore."

"Rough time, huh?"

"You got that right. Megan and I fought all the time. It was a bad situation, but I figured out a way to make it worse."

"John. You don't have to tell me. . . "

"It's okay. I probably need to talk about it."

"Only if you want to."

"I want to. Our school had its annual fundraising gala. The trustees held the affair at a big downtown Denver hotel. The men wore black ties and the woman wore sparkly gowns. All the faculty and their spouses attended. So did all the board members and their spouses."

"Sounds pretty uptown."

"It was. I spent most of the time at the bar, shooting the breeze with our football coach about West Haven's chances to repeat as conference champs that year. Until I spotted Owen Baldwin stroking Megan's arm at a table in the far corner of the ballroom."

"And something snapped," Jackie said.

"Big time. Baldwin and I had words. The words turned personal. He kept reminding me how much money he had. He told me my wife didn't love me anymore. Told me how much she loved him. I added a few choice words of my own. Then he shoved me. I shoved him back. Like a couple of kids on the playground. Then he took a swing at me. That's when I lost it. Let's just say what happened next was like something out of an old cowboy movie. He landed in the middle of a table of other trustees and their wives and wound up with a broken collarbone, a fractured jaw and a busted nose. His buddies had to pull me off of him or I would have killed him."

"Whoa."

"The whole thing got recorded on somebody's phone camera and got posted on YouTube. It didn't exactly go viral, but every teacher, parent and administrator and every board member at West Haven saw what I did. Over and over, in slow motion.

There was talk of early dementia or delayed PTSD from the war. I heard the term "anger management" enough to last a lifetime. The school insisted I take early retirement. Megan divorced me. Baldwin got the district attorney to come after me. They were golfing buddies. The DA and I cut a deal. Leave Colorado forever or face jail time for assault. Susan invited me down here. The party was over in Denver."

Jackie shook her head. "Damn. That's a hell of a story. It sounds like you can be a real bear when you get riled up."

I blew a raspberry. "Actually, I'm a pretty gentle soul. A good book and a roaring fire do me fine."

"A gentle giant?"

"I hope so. But I guess we all do what we have to do. It's what makes us human."

I could see relief wash over Jackie like an ocean wave. "Thanks. I thought you might... you know... Think I was awful. Being a stripper with no education."

"I could never think you were awful," I said. "Truth be told, I think you're pretty wonderful."

Jackie's smile was radiant. "I think you're pretty wonderful too." She threw her arms around my neck and pulled me close, locking me in a tight embrace. I put my arms around her and pulled her even closer. She rested her head on my shoulder and we just stood that way for a couple of minutes.

When we let go, Jackie and I looked into each other's eyes. "Let's go find those kids," she said, still smiling.

CHAPTER 42

THE HOUSE WAS ON FIRE. Gray-black smoke seeped into the room as Susan hobbled across the bedroom and put her hand on the door. The wood was too hot to touch. The smell of burning wood grew stronger and stronger. The greatest hits of the 80s went silent.

She was going to die.

This was how it was going to end. *Susan Coffman, 42, a local realtor, burned to death in the picturesque Cromwell Mansion on Coastline Road. She was the mother of two and was active in the local Libertarian Party. The source of the fire remains unknown.*

Unknown my ass, Susan thought. The murderous twins had set the house on fire out of sheer meanness when they left. And now that meanness was going to cost Susan her life.

She looked out of the gaping hole in the bedroom wall. The wind was so strong she had to hold on to what was left of the enclosure to keep from being blown off her feet. Beyond the flooded road, the crashing waves of the Gulf pounded the beach. She looked down at the circular driveway that ran right under the bedroom. She pictured herself jumping, landing on the driveway and then rolling like an acrobat. Only she always flunked PE in school. Besides, the drop was too far. The concrete drive was too hard. She pictured her head hitting the concrete and bursting open like a watermelon.

She battled the urge to collapse on the floor in a heap and cry and wail at her fate. But that wasn't going to help the situation. Susan Coffman was a fighter and she intended to fight.

First things first. Her ankle had swollen to twice its normal size and she needed something to help her get around. Hopping on one foot she made her way into the bedroom's massive walk-in closet. The closet smelled of wet wool and masculine cologne. Rows of expensive suits and sport coats lined the wall and a dozen pairs of polished shoes filled the floor beneath the suits.

She spotted a set of golf clubs in a dark blue golf bag in the rear of the closet. Just what the doctor ordered.

The smell of scorched wood grew stronger.

Susan selected a nine iron. Perfect. Using the head as a handle, the golf club could serve as a makeshift cane. She could put her weight on the club instead of her ankle and move around without so much pain.

Back in the bedroom, the smoke was billowing under the door and the burning odor was becoming overpowering. The house was burning down and she had to get out or die.

She thought about jumping again. Still too risky. Her eyes frantically scanned the bedroom.

An idea occurred to her. It was far from perfect and fraught with danger, but it beat the hell out of burning alive or splattering on the driveway. The plan was something out of a Nancy Drew novel, but what the hell, it worked for Nancy Drew.

Hobbling around on her golf club cane, Susan flipped back the covers on the king-sized bed. She stripped the sheets, rolled them length-wise and tied the ends together.

The door burst into flame and waves of heat washed over Susan, causing her to let out a cry of fear.

Moving as fast as her ankle would let her, she tied one end of the sheet ladder around the mammoth leg of an antique armoire. She didn't know one knot from another so a square knot had to suffice. Fortunately, the knot didn't have to hold for long.

An earsplitting crash echoed from the interior of the house below. Susan guessed that the upstairs landing was burning and had crashed to the floor below. She didn't have much time.

She tossed the sheet-ladder out of the hole in the bedroom wall. The sheet blew sideways in the lashing wind and the end came up short of the driveway by a couple of feet. But she thought her plan was still workable. She shuffled back into the bedroom, grabbed her purse and tossed her bag and the golf club through the opening in the wall.

Her heart pounded in her chest like a bass drum. She was not athletic despite her father's numerous attempts to sign her up for soccer leagues and softball teams. Basically, she hated physical activity. But she was determined.

Susan seized the sheet-ladder with both hands and eased her way through the opening. She had never repelled, but that seemed like the best plan under the circumstances. Holding on to the sheet, she balanced her good foot against the side of the house, pushed off, let her hands slide down the ladder and then catch herself with her foot when the ladder swung back into the house.

Then she did it again. And again.

Until a powerful wind caught her and blew her far to the left.

The sudden gust caught her off guard and her grip slipped on the sheet. She frantically reached upward with her left hand and tried to steady herself by grabbing the sheet above her.

But the gale spun her around and around. Her right hand began to lose its hold on the sheet as her body spun out of control.

Then something jerked her neck upward, causing a searing pain and cutting off her wind. She clutched at her neck and made a terrifying discovery. Somehow the sheet-ladder had gotten tangled up in her bandana and turned the scarf into a hangman's noose.

Her mind raced. They weren't going to find Susan's burnt body in the Cromwell mansion. They were going to find her hanging by the neck outside the second story window.

Her strangled throat began to gurgle as she gasped for precious oxygen. Her right hand screamed in pain and begged to let go of the sheet, but Susan knew that if she released her hold that would be the end and she would be left hanging by the neck from her lucky bandana.

She doggedly clung to the sheet, struggling to pull herself upward to lessen the strangle hold on her throat. Her left hand abandoned its futile search for the sheet and fumbled for the knot in her bandana. When she found it, she seized the end flap and pulled with all her strength.

At first the knot refused to yield, but gradually it loosened and finally came untied.

As life-giving air rushed into her throat, she slipped a few feet down the sheet but then steadied herself with her left hand, which had found the sheet above her head.

One more repel off the wall and she let go of the sheet and landed on the driveway.

She lost her balance when her swollen right foot hit the pavement and she tumbled over. But she was out of the burning house and safe from the hangman's noose.

Now there was no time to waste.

Her ankle screamed and Susan let out a moan as she crawled across the driveway and retrieved her golf club and her purse. She had parked her Range Rover in one of the slots in front of the five-car garage but the top and sides of her vehicle were caked with sea salt.

Susan slid behind the wheel. She always kept the car key in her pocket. She said a short prayer and pushed the starter button. The Range Rover's engine coughed and surged into life.

"Thank you! Thank You!" Susan said out loud.

She threw the Range Rover into reverse and tried to step on the accelerator. But her swollen right ankle rebelled. She scooted over as far as she could go in the bucket seat and gently pressed on the pedal with her left foot. The car lurched and bucked out onto the driveway.

She looked up at the Cromwell mansion, where flames danced through the hole in the bedroom wall and flickered through the windows on both floors. Black smoke hurdled skyward. "Oh, God." Susan shoved back against a surging sense of despair. "That beautiful house."

Susan carefully pulled away from the burning building, experimenting with the unnatural left footed driving stance.

She started down the highway, dodging abandoned cars and giant tree limbs and anger seized her as she thought about the murderous twins finding Rand and Skylar at the mall. She pressed on the accelerator. Her babies were in danger but Mama was on the way.

Fortunately, the Emerald Fields Mall was not that far away. One of the selling points of the Cromwell mansion was that, even though the house was located on the Gulf, the place offered easy access to one of the Emerald Coast's showcase shopping areas. Take the coastal road to Seminole Drive. Then straight north to the mall. Fifteen minutes tops.

But Seminole Drive was under water. The surrounding land had turned into a small lake and removed the shortcut to the mall with it.

Susan remained undaunted. Thanks to her real estate business, she knew the Bay St. Edwards peninsula as well as anyone and Farm Road #4 paralleled Seminole Drive and circled by the western end of the mall.

The farm road was covered with water, but it was passable in the Range Rover. Susan kept her left foot on the accelerator and the SUV surged through the flood waters, leaving a wake behind the tires.

Although Susan had used the farm road as a cut-through numerous times, the surrounding land looked totally unfamiliar. Buildings were gone, trees had vanished and most of the land was submerged under brownish flood water.

Desperate for news of her children, Susan fumbled in her purse for her smartphone. As she swiped the bottom of the screen, she could almost hear her father's oft spoken, nagging admonition. "Please, Susan. Don't text and drive. You never know what's going to happen. A child could run out in front of you, a car could pull out of a side road. Texting while you drive is stupid. Don't to it."

Well, there certainly weren't any children on Farm Road #4 and there were no other cars on the horizon, so she swiped the phone with a vengeance. Her father was Old School and he never seemed to understand that busy people like Susan had to take advantage of every moment. It was the 21st century and this was how people lived.

She hit Skylar's number and listened to the haunting silence.

The Range Rover swerved across the deserted road. Susan jerked the car back into the right lane. When she looked back at the left lane, she realized how close she had come to disaster.

The under-side of the farm road on the left lane had collapsed and water had surged under the highway, eaten away the earth beneath it and the road had given way in random patches the size of kitchen counters. If Susan's tires had slipped passed the edge, the Range Rover would have flipped over.

Susan bit down on her lip and punched Rand's number on the cellphone but nothing happened. No beeps. No static. Nothing but quiet.

The inability to use her phone left Susan feeling more lost and alone than anything else that had happened to her in the last twenty-four hours. Her phone was her life. Without it, she was cut off from all humanity. Abandoned on a lonely farm road that was disintegrating before her eyes.

She turned on the car radio but station after station delivered nothing but static. The world Susan knew was gone. She pounded the dashboard in anger and frustration.

Susan Coffman had always believed in a rational, ordered universe. A world where hard work and perseverance paid dividends. An understandable world where, if you played by the rules, you won.

Now there were no rules. Only chaos and madness. Life had become unpredictable and terrifying. Susan had lost control.

CHAPTER 43

ANOTHER HALF MILE BROUGHT US to the intersection of a major roadway. The bad news was the Gulf of Mexico lay on the other side of the highway.

"Damn," Jackie said. "We went the wrong way. I thought we were heading north, but we must have gotten turned around. Sorry."

"Not your fault." I tried to hide my disappointment. "It was my hunch that took us down this road." And that was really stupid, I thought. I should have known better. I mean I was in the infantry and I was trained to deal with these kinds of situations.

All of a sudden, I felt a storm of anger and frustration building up inside of me. Skylar and Rand were trapped in the mall and I couldn't get to them. I was so tired that I just wanted to lay down in the middle of the road. But I had to keep going. I had to get to the mall and save my grandchildren. Failure was not an option.

Jackie stopped and planted her hands on her hips, studying the landscape. She seemed as disappointed as I was. "Nothing looks familiar," she said. "Let's take a right and follow the water. The next intersection is bound to be heading north toward the mall."

It seemed like a hell of a lot better idea than mine had been so we started down the highway. The storm inside of me abated. I didn't have time for frustration and recriminations. I had to get a job done.

A couple of hundred yards later, I noticed a change in the air. "Do you smell something different?" I said.

Jackie took a deep breath. "Yeah. I smell smoke. Smoke and something else."

"Yeah. What in the world? And look up there." A pair of vultures lazily circled the beach.

I scanned the shoreline. "Look on the other side of those dunes. That looks like purple smoke." The smoke billowed over the sandy shore and disappeared into the gray sky.

We crossed the muddy shoulder of the road and found a path between a pair of dunes. On the other side, the pathway dropped downward toward the beach and the source of the odd smelling smoke.

Jackie and I froze the minute we saw what was happening on the beach below us.

The same refrigerator truck I had seen at the beachcomber's house off Highway 72 was parked on the shoreline. A few feet from the truck, a half dozen uniformed cops, hidden behind surgical masks, placed body bags in a neat row as they came off the truck.

The corpses were decomposing in various stages and the hot, humid air reeked with the stench of rotting flesh. The vultures circled lower.

"Oh, my god!" Jackie's hand went to her mouth. "What are we looking at? What the hell is this?"

I shook my head, too stunned to speak. I desperately wanted to get to the Emerald Fields Mall and find the kids, but I couldn't take my eyes off what was happening on the beach.

Two more masked cops picked up the bags from the end of the row, hauled them across the beach and tossed them into a gigantic bonfire.

"They're disposing of those corpses like rubbish," I said. "They wouldn't treat hurricane victims that way. What is this?"

"Maybe the cops could help us get to the mall."

At that moment, I spotted Chief Brunson by the side of the truck, scanning the waters of the Gulf with a pair of binoculars.

"I don't think that's a good idea," I said. "I think these cops are on some kind of bizarre mission. I don't think they're interested in helping anybody."

"But they're cops. They have to help us."

"You would think."

The smell of the pyre of burning corpses grew stronger as the ochre colored smoke from the bonfire spiraled into the sky.

Suddenly, Chief Brunson pivoted away from the water and did a sweep of the beach and the dunes with his binoculars. He froze when he saw Jackie and me on the edge of the path.

"We need to get out of here," I said. "Fast. We're witnessing something that nobody was supposed to see."

"Copy that," Jackie said. "I'm really getting scared. This is the creepiest thing I've ever seen. I can't get out of here fast enough. Let's go."

I took her hand and we retreated through the dunes, back to the highway.

I pushed my aching hip to its limits, limping down the coastline road. The stench of the burning bodies chased us for several yards. Fortunately, no one else did.

After what we had seen, neither one of us felt like talking. We hustled down the highway until we were both out of breath, then we slowed our pace. The Gulf raged on our left and we passed piles of rubble that used to be houses on our right. Every few steps, I glanced over my shoulder.

A half an hour later, we ran into another intersection. The new road looked like it had once been a major thoroughfare and had less water covering it than the coastal road.

"We may have caught some luck," Jackie said. "If this highway is Monaco Avenue, which I think it is, it goes straight up to the Emerald Fields Mall."

We searched the area for street signs, but they were long gone.

"Let's give it a shot," I said. "But we've got to hurry."

"I hear you."

I paused for a second and looked back down the coastal road. There was no one in sight. As we headed north, the wind picked up, adding to the sense of desolation that hung over the intersection. A pair of rogue vultures circled directly over us. Talk about a bad omen.

"I need to tell you something," Jackie said, as we passed the wreckage of a tiny strip mall.

"Sure. Fire away." Jackie had been distant and withdrawn since we witnessed the cops burning the corpses and I was glad she was talking again.

"I might know what the cops back there are doing on the beach."

“You’re kidding.” I had been racking my brain, trying to figure out why in the world the local police force would be burning dead bodies on the beach rather than helping the survivors of a vicious hurricane.

“I hope I’m wrong,” Jackie said in a low voice. “You remember I told you about the dive out on the highway where I used to work. It’s closer to Crystal City than to Bay St. Edwards.”

I nodded.

“A couple of Bay St. Edwards cops were regulars. They came in once or twice a week. Out of uniform. They both drank like fish. Shots with beer chasers. Both of them liked to talk.”

“What did they talk about?”

Jackie sighed and shook her head. “About a year ago, they talked a lot about this Cuban guy. Guy named Cholo. He was some kind of union organizer. One of the cops told me Cholo was going around talking to the migrant laborers up and down the Emerald Coast. They said he wanted to unionize all the workers on the new condos and strip malls as well as the agricultural workers. The cops said he was like Caesar Chávez. Quiet but dynamic. They said he was making some headway.”

“And they didn’t like it.”

“Not a bit. They were getting pressure from the big citrus growers. Pressure from the tourist people. Pressure from the developers. The last thing the tourist industry wanted was a lot of bad publicity about unhappy migrant workers on the coast. Cholo was talking strike.”

“I’m not surprised,” I said. “The life of a migrant worker has got to be the pits.”

"Amen to that." Jackie picked up her pace. Telling me about Cholo and the cops seemed to energize her and it was all I could do to keep up the pace.

"Anyway, Cholo had something of an organization. About a dozen or so Cubans. They all went around to the migrant camps. Talked union. Talked about a big strike. The papers and the TV people got wind of it."

"What are you saying?"

"One of cops at the club told me the growers and tourist people hit the panic button. They thought angry immigrant labor would damage the reputation of the Emerald Coast. The cops were scared Cholo and his people might do something that would go viral on YouTube. Nobody wanted any part of something like that. It would cost the towns on the Emerald Coast a fortune."

"I can imagine."

"Okay," Jackie said. "Here's the kicker. About three months ago, Cholo and his guys dropped off the map. Nothing in the papers. Nothing on TV. You just didn't hear about them anymore. Then the two Bay St. Edwards cops came into the club. Got absolutely wasted. At first, they didn't mention Cholo. Their lips were sealed until. . ."

"Until what?"

"Until one of them mentioned Cholo's name and the other one blurted out something like 'we took care of that bastard.' His partner came out of his chair, grabbed his buddy and drug him out of the club. I never saw them again."

Assuming Jackie was right, you didn't need to be Sherlock Holmes to put together a scenario of what we had witnessed on the beach. Hurricane Atlas had uncovered a bunch of bodies the cops thought would be buried forever and now Chief Brunson and his men were scrambling to get rid of them. Still that was pretty far-fetched. "You don't think. . ."

"That's exactly what I think," Jackie said. "I think we may have just seen the remains of Cholo and his guys go up in smoke."

CHAPTER 44

SUSAN'S FIRST SIGHT OF THE Emerald Fields Mall drew an anguished cry of despair. She had shopped at the mall for years, dropped the kids off at the Cineplex for movies, bought take-out from the Panda Express, purchased clothes at the boutique shops. The mall had always been a familiar anchor in Susan's adult life.

Until now.

She eased the Range Rover into the parking lot and brought the car to a bumpy stop, taking in the frightening spectacle in front of her. The parking lot was filled with overturned cars, piles of twisted metal and wood debris. The hurricane had peeled off the roof of the mall like a giant tin can. Hugh strips of roofing littered the walkway to the entrance and yellow fiberglass installation panels dotted the lot. Sheet metal wall panels lay crumbled across the fountain.

Susan inched her SUV through an obstacle course of downed tree branches, light poles and upside-down automobiles and pulled the Range Rover next to a pick-up truck that was resting on its side and stopped. She was as close to the mall as she was going to get. When she thought about what Rand and Skylar must have been through, her eyes filled with tears.

She grabbed her purse and struggled out of the driver's seat, trying to protect her injured ankle. Malls were usually brightly lighted, cheerful, inviting places but now the Emerald Fields Mall was as dark as a tomb.

An unnatural silence surrounded the place. There was no one in sight and no car sounds. No birds. Nothing but a silent, fog-shrouded world. Susan hobbled on her golf club cane around a pile of rubble, heading for the entrance. Then she stopped in her tracks. A pair of mud-splattered ATVs sat parked in front of the foyer.

The twins had beaten her to Emerald Fields. Rand and Skylar were trapped somewhere inside the mall with a pair of psychotic killers. Confronted with crisis, Susan did what she always did. She whipped out her smartphone. She punched Skylar's number but the phone was still dead. Her options had run out. She had to go into the mall and save her babies. She had to regain control.

Although it was only late afternoon, the low hanging clouds made it feel like night might descend at any moment.

Susan went back to the mall entrance but discovered that she couldn't get to the glass doors because of the piles of rubble and debris that had landed on the walkway. With no other choice, she followed the curve of the building, searching for another way in. The windows of every store were either boarded up or blown out. The hurricane had apparently exploded on the Emerald Fields Mall like a bomb.

Half way around the building, she found an opening in a shattered display window of a sporting goods store. Using her golf club crutch, she knocked aside jagged glass fragments until there was a hole large enough for her to crawl through.

The floodwaters inside the darkening store reached Susan's calves and crossing the store to get inside the mall proved to be a slow process. Part of the ceiling of the sporting goods store had collapsed and wires and metal beams dangled precariously from above. Baseball caps, catcher's mitts, NFL and NBA jerseys, fishing rods and basketballs bobbed in the flood waters.

The doors to the mall interior were open and Susan hobbled on her cane as fast as she could into the lower floor. The whole mall was deserted. The only sound was the lapping of the floodwaters. Susan scanned the interior in search of the murderous twins but the entire floor appeared uninhabited.

Skylar had said that she and her brother were trapped in a costume store on the second floor, so Susan made her way to an escalator in the center of the mall.

As she rounded a large concrete planter, she let out a cry. A dead body floated motionless in the floodwater. The corpse was face down, a young woman, her long blonde hair splayed out in front of her. Susan had a nightmarish flash of the body being Skylar, but quickly realized the woman was much larger and older than her daughter. The sour taste of vomit filled her mouth. How could her ordered world have come so unglued?

The escalator had died without power, but it offered a staircase to the top floor and Susan climbed the metal stairs slowly and painfully, using her golf club to support her injured ankle.

By the time she reached the second floor, she was gasping for breath. She paused at the top of the escalator and scanned the second floor for signs of life. She didn't see any.

HURRICANE ATLAS HAD HURLED A thick tree trunk through the roof and now the uprooted tree blocked the entrance to a department store. The storm had hurled a white van through the front window of a shoe store and shards of glass from shattered store windows carpeted the mall's walkways. A grayish light poured through the hole where the roof had been and the salty scent of the Gulf offered the only relief from the decaying stench of the floodwaters.

Susan vaguely remembered the costume shop being somewhere at the far end of the top floor. She wove her way around overturned planters and downed tree branches. The floor was wet, but not flooded and her nine-iron enabled her to move down the row of shops with a minimum of discomfort to her ankle.

A sudden wave of dizziness forced her to lean on one of the planters. Only it wasn't dizziness. The floor was moving, shifting to her left. The moving was accompanied by a metallic groaning sound that was slowly increasing in intensity. It was a grinding echo like two cars rubbing against each other.

"Oh, my god," Susan whispered as the reality of the situation hit her. The entire structure of the mall's interior had been compromised by the hurricane. The second-story floor could collapse at any second. She clung to a concrete planter like a drowning woman on a life raft in a raging sea.

After a couple of minutes, the grinding sound receded and the floor seemed to steady itself.

When the swaying floor grew still, she caught sight of movement at the far end of the mall, causing her to suck in a quick breath. Moving a few feet closer, she crouched behind a pile of girders and loose boards that had fallen from the ceiling during the hurricane.

She peeked out from the side of a girder and her heart sank. The twins were trying to break into the Drug Rite across the upper walkway from the Halloween costume shop. "Oh, no. Please," Susan muttered.

The twins weren't having any luck getting into the drug store.

The glass front of the Drug Rite was intact and the metal caging that sealed off the store at night had been pulled across the front. Susan assumed some conscientious store employee had taken the precaution of locking up the store to prevent looting after the hurricane.

The twin in the army field hat gripped the bars of the metal covering with both hands like a man in jail. He rattled the cage with all his strength, but the bars refused to yield. He continued to shake the immovable barrier even though it was apparent nothing was going to happen.

Finally, he let out an animal shriek of frustration and sank to his knees, holding on to the bars, peering into the drug store beyond.

His brother, who had been standing behind him, attacked the bars with a chain, lashing them more out of frustration than hope that he could gain entrance to the Drug Rite. The metallic clanging echoed through the deserted mall.

The twin in the army field hat howled and screamed as if he was in the throes of some horrible agony.

The other twin let out a long string of swear words, grabbed the bars and pulled and pushed them with all his strength. The gate clanged but didn't budge. Anguish filled the young man's face and he whirled around, placed his back against the gate, sliding downward into a sitting position in a gesture of defeat.

As the twin's yowling and yelling subsided, the top floor of the mall grew quiet. Susan held her breath and her eyes locked on the Halloween costume store across the way from the Drug Rite. That was her destination. Skylar and Rand were in the shop.

Suddenly, the floor began to sway and the metallic groaning started again.

CHAPTER 45

JACKIE AND I SLOGGED DOWN the center of the flooded road. My backpack was starting to pinch my shoulder and my hip was sending out SOS signals for more ibuprofen. But it was easy to ignore the pain because my mind was reeling.

What on earth had we just witnessed? Could it really have been Bay St. Edwards cops burning the dead bodies of a bunch of Cuban rabble-rousers? How was that even possible? And if that was what we had seen, what should we do about it? Who could we report it to? Who was in charge?

I tried to drive the images of the burning bodies out of my mind and focus on the task at hand. Jackie was convinced the road we were traveling ended at the Mall and she knew the territory far better than I did, so I just hoped and prayed I had enough gas left in the tank to get there.

The road swung to the right and on the other side of the bend was a cemetery.

The hurricane played no favorites—rich or poor, alive or dead, Hurricane Atlas had attacked with unabandoned savagery. The storm had roared through the resting place of the dead, its vicious winds ripping tombstones out of the ground and scattering them in all directions. Wherever the flood waters hit, the impact had uprooted coffins, ripped them open and tossed their grisly contents all over the grounds.

The scene made the paintings of Hieronymus Bosch look like Mickey Mouse cartoons.

"How ya holding up, slugger?" Jackie said.

I managed a grin. "Never felt better." I let out a small sigh. "Well, maybe a few times."

"Or a few thousand," Jackie added. "We've made it this far and. . ." She froze in mid-sentence. "Do you hear something?"

I shook my head. "Jackie. Truth be told, I need a hearing aid. Bad. There could be a herd of stampeding elephants around the next bend and I probably wouldn't hear them."

"It's okay," Jackie said. "But I thought I heard. . . wait a minute. There it is again."

I strained to hear whatever it was but all I heard was the wind whistling in my ears.

"It's someone crying. They're inside the cemetery. Somewhere over there." Jackie pointed to a small rise.

"May we should go look," I said, although I was really getting impatient to get to the mall and find the kids.

"You're a good man," Jackie said. "A good man with a good heart. Let's check it out."

Since Jackie could hear the crying, I let her lead the way through the hole in the fence and over the rise. We tiptoed around a couple of skeletons and a pair of overturned coffins. The uprooted graves were already filling up with water.

When we reached the top of the rise, I was relieved to see that the section of the cemetery below the ridge was relatively untouched by the storm. Most of the trees were still intact except for one giant oak that had been displaced and flung across the narrow access road that cut through the boneyard.

What startled me was the sight of a uniformed cop, sitting cross-legged in front of a tombstone, his hands covering his face while he rocked back and forth, sobbing uncontrollably.

"Should we bother him?" Jackie asked.

I shrugged. "Tough call. Maybe we could help. I hate to just leave him in the aftermath of the hurricane. He may be hurt or disoriented."

Jackie nodded her agreement.

"Excuse me, officer," I said as we approached the man from behind. "Are you okay? Is there anything we can do to help?"

The cop took his hands away from his face and slowly turned around to face us. He was a young guy, in his late twenties. He either needed a shave or was sporting one of those trendy three-day beards young men seemed so fond of.

His face was a portrait of agony, his eyes rimmed an ugly bright red, his mouth turned down, his lower lip trembling uncontrollably.

He seemed surprise to see us.

"If we could help you, we'd be glad. . ."

"Who are you?" His hand went to the pistol strapped on his hip.

"Just a couple of hurricane survivors," I said. "We're on our way to the Emerald Fields Mall. My grandchildren are trapped there."

The cop looked puzzled like he didn't understand what I had just said.

"We'd be glad to help you," Jackie said. "If there's anything we could do. . ."

"No one can help me." The cop struggled to kept his voice from breaking. "I've done a terrible thing. An awful, horrible thing. Not even God can forgive me. No one can help me. Not now. Not ever."

I slipped off my backpack and put it on the ground. "The hurricane was the last straw," the cop said. "It was God's message to me. He knows what I did." He drew his knees up under his chin and started shaking. "I came here to ask Cindy to forgive me, but she won't. She's ashamed of me."

I looked at the tombstone. The ledger read *Cynthia R. Robbins. 1985-2010. Beloved Wife and Mother.*

"What's your name, son?" I kept my voice low.

"Rollins. Josh Rollins." He wiped his nose on his sleeve.

"Was Cindy your wife?"

A tiny smile crept into the corners of his mouth. "Yeah. We were only married three years. And three months. Then she died. Ovarian cancer. She was too young to go. I mean, our lives had just started. And she died. Right after that, I lost my way. I started drinking and doing. . . really bad things."

Jackie got down on her knees and draped an arm over the young man's shoulder. "You're in shock, Josh. We've all just been through a horrible trauma. But we're okay. We're all gonna make it. We're gonna survive. I promise."

Rollins shook his head. "Not me. I'm done. I'm done with all of it. All I want to do is stay here with my Cindy."

"I understand," Jackie said. "But you're welcome to come with us." She looked up at me and I nodded my approval.

"It's over," Rollins sobbed. "It's all over. My Cindy is gone. Our house blew away in the storm. Chief Brunson wants to kill me. I can't go back to work."

"Chief Brunson?" I got down on my knees next to Jackie. "Josh. We're you involved in burning the bodies on the beach?"

Rollins looked up, his eyes wide saucers of surprise. "Yeah. We all were. All the Bay St. Edwards cops. The hurricane exposed the bodies. Chief Brunson said we had to get rid of them before the state cops or the National Guard got on the peninsula. I couldn't stand what we were doing. I mean those men were dead just like Cindy and we treated them like sacks of garbage. That was plain wrong. I told Chief Brunson I was out. I mean, we all swore we'd never tell anyone but the chief thought I might crack and rat out all the guys. That's when I turned and ran. I kept running until I got here. With Cindy. Where I belong."

"It's gonna be alright, Josh. Hang in there." Jackie gave Rollins a gentle hug.

I felt so sorry for the young cop. His whole life had come apart in ways I could only imagine.

But I had to know. "Josh. Are they burning the bodies of a guy known as Cholo and some of his fellow Cubans?"

Rollins burst into a fit of sobbing and wailing. Then he managed to pull himself together enough to release something that had been locked up inside of him for a long time. His tale was interspersed with intermediate crying fits.

"Yeah. Cholo. That was the guy's name. He was stirring up a lot of trouble all over the coast. A few months after Cindy passed, these developers from Crystal City put out a bounty on Cholo. It was all hush-hush. They told Chief Brunson if he could make Cholo disappear, it would be worth a shitload of money."

"The developers offered to pay the police to kill Cholo and the others?" I could believe what I was hearing.

"Yeah. Our department only has a dozen guys. Most of them are terrible racist. They especially hate Hispanics. Even the black cops hate them. Everybody fell in line."

"So then what happened?"

Rollins looked back at his wife's grave. "Oh, Cindy. I'm so sorry. You were gone and I missed you so much. I just went along. Oh, God. I'm so sorry."

"All of you were in on it?" I asked.

"Yeah. The whole force. We rounded up all the Cubans at this bar one night. Put them all in a patty wagon. Drove them out to Shadow Cove, marched them out to the beach. It was the middle of the night and there was no one around. So we lined up the Cubans and shot them. Like a firing squad. A week later, Chief Brunson called me into his office and gave a big envelope full of cash. New bills. Almost a year's salary. He made me swear I'd never tell anybody what happened. I felt awful and dirty, but I took the money. Cindy would have been so ashamed of me." Rollins was overcome by another wave of sobs and agonizing cries.

I didn't know what to do. I had seen guys like Rollins in Southeast Asia. Young soldiers who got overwhelmed with what they witnessed and lost it. Some of them made a recovery. Some of them never came back.

Rollins wiped his face on the back of his sleeve. "Then, this morning," he stammered through deep breaths of fresh air. "The

Chief notified all of us. We had to report to South Bay where we buried the Cubans. The wind had lashed the beach and uncovered them. We loaded the bodies in the truck and took them all the way out to Magnet Cove. We built a fire and started tossing the corpses on it But one of the body bags split open and I saw what was inside. It was awful. It was like nothing I had ever seen before. I got sick. I couldn't do it anymore. So, I walked away. Chief Brunson yelled at me, but I didn't care. I started running and didn't stop until I got here."

Jackie grimaced. "Come with us, Josh. Please. The mall's just a few minutes away. You can help us find the kids and then will figure out what to do next to get out of this nightmare. You could tell your story to someone in authority."

Rollins shook his head. "I can't leave. I won't leave. You people seem really nice, but I would only slow you down. I'm not myself."

I realized there was nothing we could say to change poor Rollins' mind. He was too far gone.

"Okay," I said. "When we find help. The National Guard or somebody, we'll come back for you. I promise."

Rollins nodded. "That sounds good. But whatever you do, don't trust any of the Bay St. Edwards cops. Their butts are on the line and they're libel to do anything. If their secret ever gets out. . ."

"I understand," I said, struggling to my feet. "We hate to leave you, but I see where you're coming from." I extended my hand and Josh shook it. Then I helped Jackie stand up. She brushed the dirt and mud off her pants.

Rollins looked up at us. "This is where I want to be," he said. His voice was barely audible.

Jackie and I turned and headed toward the hole in the cemetery fence and the road to the mall. We were both too stunned to talk.

We crawled through the hole in the fence and headed down the flooded street. We made it about twenty yards when we heard a single gunshot echoing from the cemetery.

CHAPTER 46

"THERE IT IS! THE EMERALD Fields Mall!" Jackie raised her fist in a victory salute as we emerged into a clearing on the west side of the mall.

Without thinking, in my hurry to find Rand and Skylar, I tried to run the rest of the way. Bad move. How many years had it been since I had actually run? My last 10K had been a decade ago. And that was jogging. The first two steps toward the mall felt like someone had hammered a nail into my hip. It was all I could do to keep from crying out in pain.

As much as I wanted to get to the kids, my running days were long gone.

Jackie came up behind me and we stood in the clearing and caught our breath. I held up my hand and we exchanged an enthusiastic high five. Then we embraced out of relief and joy. We had made it. Hurricanes, burning corpses, nothing had stopped us.

But the journey had taken its toll. Jackie looked exhausted. Dark circles rimmed her eyes and the bounce had gone out of her step. But I locked eyes with her and saw strength in the woman's soul. We had one more task and both of us were determined to pull it off.

I started limping across the parking lot as fast as my hip would let me and Jackie fell in step. My thoughts briefly wondered back to the scene in the cemetery. I was sure young patrolman Rollins had ended his life and I honestly didn't blame him. Tormented by the loss of his young wife, the man had committed murder. He was an officer of the law and I knew what he had done would have haunted him the rest of life.

I also knew that as soon as we found some semblance of authority, we had to tell them about what the Bay St. Edwards cops had done to Cholo and his men. But now we had to take care of the task at hand, which was getting into the Emerald Fields Mall and finding Rand and Skylar.

"I was hoping the National Guard helicopters could land in the parking lot," I said. "But now, I don't know. Look at all that crap."

"I don't think a helicopter could land anywhere around here," Jackie said. "Overturned cars, tree trucks, pieces of the mall roof. Damn, John. You and I are lucky to be alive."

"That's what I tell myself every morning. Far from over."

Jackie grinned.

We made our way through the wreckage in the parking lot, hundreds of dead birds lay scattered over the asphalt expanse.

"What a mess," Jackie said as we approached the entrance to the mall. "I don't think we can get inside this way. All that junk is blocking the door."

I only half heard her. My attention had been diverted by a pair of ATVs parked at the side of the entrance. A chill ran down my spine. I remembered the scene at Mike's Motorcycles. Poor Mike had been crushed by an ATV. And I remembered the ATV tracks at the

Dragon Hill mansion, where we found the dead couple in the pantry. My heart started racing. What the hell were we dealing with?

"We need to be extra careful," I said, indicating the ATVs. "I'm getting a bad vibe about this place."

"I hear you. But we've got to find another way into the mall."

"Right. But let's find it fast. I think the kids are in serious danger." I glanced over my shoulder at the ATVs and the nerves in my body went on high alert like I was back in the jungles of Southeast Asia.

We hike around the exterior of the mall, past piles of wreckage and scummy pools of water. Finally, we spotted a door marked "Employees Only" next to a department store. Atlas had blown the door off its hinges and what was left of the door dangled over the entrance at a precarious angle.

We slipped through the doorway and crossed the main floor of the department store, wading through stinking brown floodwater.

The interior of the Emerald Fields Mall looked like something out of an old science fiction movie. The marquee of the Cineplex had fallen to the floor and shattered. The escalator across from the department store was blocked by a twisted and smashed Cadillac Escalade that Atlas had apparently dropped through the hole that had once been the roof of the mall.

"We need to get up to the second floor," I said.

"We can't get up that escalator," Jackie said. "It's blocked with all that junk. Maybe there's another one at the other end of the mall."

"Sounds good, but let's hurry." I looked down the vast expanse of the flooded floor space and let out a sigh. The last mile of a marathon was always the hardest.

Fortunately, I spotted a door marked "Emergency Stairway" on the other side of the Verizon store. "Let's give that a shot."

"Way to go, Eagle Eye."

I pulled the door open and was greeted by a totally dark cavern. "No electricity. No lights."

"That's the way it works," Jackie said.

I pulled off my backpack and dug through the contents until I found my flashlight. I flicked on the beam and aimed it up the stairwell. "Be prepared. That's what the Boy Scouts used to say."

"Were you a good Boy Scout?"

"Not that good."

I led the way up the stairs, sweeping the flashlight beam in front of me. The stairwell got us to the second floor of the mall.

I pushed the stairway door outward and stepped into the wasteland that had once been the second floor of the Emerald Fields Mall.

My excitement at finding the kids mounted with each step as Jackie and I wove our way around the junk. When we reached the end of the walkway, Jackie froze. "John, is it just my imagination or is the floor moving?"

I stopped. Jackie was right. The movement was almost imperceptible, but the floor was actually shifting.

"What the hell?" Jackie grabbed my forearm.

A groaning sound echoed through the mall, making the hairs on the back of my neck stand up. "I think the Emerald Fields Mall is about to collapse." I said. "Too much structural damage from the hurricane."

Just as I spoke, I spotted a lopsided black and orange sign hanging over the last store on the floor. 'Halloween Super Store.' A smaller sign announced "It's Not Just a Store, It's an Adventure."

CHAPTER 47

THE ENTRANCE TO THE HALLOWEEN store was blocked by a pile of boards and twisted girders. No wonder Rand and Skylar couldn't get out.

I was ready to tackle the task of clearing a path through the debris when I realized someone had beaten me to it. Whoever it was had shoved the boards aside and created a narrow tunnel to the front door of the Halloween store. Jackie and I had to turn sideways to slither past the pile of rubble on either side.

Someone had also wedged open the front door. My thoughts raced back to the ATVs parked in front of the mall. Whoever was riding around on those bikes had already done some terrible things. What if they were the ones who had tunneled into the Halloween store where my grandchildren were trapped? Could my nightmare get any worse?

We slipped into the store, where we were greeted by a snarling three headed wolf. It was a Halloween store. The wolf was made of rubber and plastic.

Beyond the wolf, we passed through a store entrance guarded by a pair of waist high gargoyles. The dim interior of the store was lighted in an odd grayish color from the hole in the roof courtesy of Atlas. The sun had all but left for the day.

"Skylar! Rand! It's Bugs! Where are you guys?" I shouted into the store.

"Bugs?" Jackie raised an eyebrow.

"It beats PeePaw," I said.

"I should say. You don't look like a PeePaw."

"Thank God."

The store was deadly silent.

"Skylar? Are you okay?" I cast the flashlight beam over shelves of Assassin Creed swords, Star Wars figures, Voodoo Queen costumes and masks of distorted ghoulish faces.

"Rand! It's Bugs! Where are you, buddy?" I looked at Jackie. My fear must have shown on my face.

"It's okay," she said. "They're probably hiding in here somewhere."

We paused in front of a shelf of plastic skulls and grinning pumpkins. When we started walking again our shoes squished with each step on the wet floor.

"Dad?"

Jackie and I froze. Susan. My relief only lasted a second. My daughter sounded terrified.

"Dad! Don't come in here! I mean it. Go and get help. Don't come any further." The voice came from somewhere in the back of the store.

There was no way I was leaving. Like a sergeant leading a jungle patrol, I motioned for Jackie to take the right side of the long shelf in front of us. She nodded her understanding. I took the left side.

I wanted to tell Jackie to bail out and go find help. To get the hell out of the store, but the look in Jackie's eyes told me she was with me to the end.

I moved to the far side of the shelf, took a deep breath and stepped into the open. Giant spiders suspended from wires danced from what was left of the ceiling. But the spiders were nothing compared to the scene in front of me.

A blond young man held Skylar from behind, his arm crooked around her throat. She struggled, twisting back and forth in the man's grip, tears streaming down her cheeks.

Rand sat on the floor, his glasses bent and crooked on his face. He was wearing a black t-shirt with yellow and red lettering on the front that said, "Lazy Butt Club." Dried blood covered the side of his cheek and his left arm was bandaged in white, gauzy cloth.

When he saw me, his face broke into a smile that radiated both relief and panic.

Susan sat cringing on the top of a black coffin crammed between two shelves of Halloween paraphernalia. She clutched her big purse to her chest. A golf club sat in her lap. Her face looked red and haggard.

Another young man in an army field hat hovered over her. My eyes darted from one man to the other. They were the same. Blond hair, buff physique, prominent noses. Twins.

The one in the field hat backhanded Susan across the face and she screamed in pain.

When I served in Vietnam, a lot of the guys in my unit took hallucinatory drugs to escape the reality of our situation. The scene in front of me felt like something unreal like those guys would have conjured up with their drug-aided imaginations. Susan sitting on a coffin, holding a golf club, twin maniacs attacking my family, giant spiders dangling from the ceiling. It had to be a hallucination.

"What the hell do you think you're doing?" My whole body had gone back over the years to the jungles of Southeast Asia. All my muscles tensed. All my nerve endings went on high alert. My heart pounded.

"Who the fuck are you?" The guy in the field hat whirled around. His face was bathed in sweat. His damp shirt clung to his back. The air felt humid and hot but nothing that would produce sweat at that level.

"What kind of people are you guys?" I slid my backpack off my shoulder and dropped it on the floor.

"Nobody invited you to the party, Gramps. Take a hike." Hat Man's eyes bulged out of his head. His mouth twitched uncontrollably.

"Stand down, son. I'm not sure you realize what you're doing here."

Hat Man's eyes flashed with anger. "Move it, Gramps. It's the apocalypse or haven't you noticed? It's the end of the world. We can do anything we want."

"Listen to me. You need some help. You're right on the edge of crazy."

"Don't call me crazy. Nobody calls me crazy."

"Then don't call me Gramps."

"You don't get it do you?" Hat Man reached down on the floor and picked up what looked like a bicycle chain. He wrapped the end of the chain around his knuckles. "We needed to get into the drug store. Get it? The drug store? Me and my brother are tapped out. No more goodies. But there's plenty in the drug store. But we can't get in. It's Armageddon and we can't get in the fuckin' drug store." His voice kept climbing higher and higher.

"Dad, get out of here." Susan looked up. A deep bruise had formed on the side of her face. "They're both insane. I saw them kill two people on the beach. They're drug addicts and they're freaking out."

Images of Mike at his motorcycle shop flashed through my mind. The severed hand on Dragon Hill. The bodies in the pantry. These guys were not just lunatics, they were cold blooded killers.

Hat Man whirled around and slammed his bicycle chain into the coffin, inches from where Susan sat. The wood splintered and flew into the air. "Shut up! Just shut up!"

"Bugs! Help!" Skylar struggled to escape the other twin's grasp. He tightened his grip on her throat until she cried out in pain.

"Don't worry, honey. This will be over in a little while." I hoped my voice sounded more confident than I felt. I stole a glance at the other end of the shelf of costumes but Jackie was nowhere in sight.

"This is gonna be over right now!" Suddenly, Hat Man lurched toward me, swing the bicycle chain over his head.

CHAPTER 48

I STEPPED BACKWARDS, LOST MY balance and grabbed the shelf to steady myself. The shelf tilted forward and a row of rubber masks—werewolves, grizzly bears, witches and bloody clowns—tumbled to the floor.

Hat Man danced around the masks. When he slowed down, I reached up on the next shelf and grabbed a plastic red and blue circular Wonder Woman shield. Clutching the shield in both hands, I held it up just in time to block a ferocious blow from the bicycle chain.

Hat Man yelled something incoherent and came at me again. I blocked a second blow with the plastic shield.

In a nanosecond, years of rage rose up inside of me and burst to the surface. The anger was not only at the pair of crazies in front of me who had assaulted my daughter and my grandchildren. It was a fury born of having to grow old and suffer all the pain and indignities that went with aging; that I had to watch wonderful old friends like Tommy Liddell die: that Hurricane Atlas had destroyed my home; that I had acted foolishly and had to leave my beloved Colorado; that the young psycho attacking me had murdered the only friend I had in Bay St. Edwards.

All of that rage raced through my veins and arteries, combining with a major adrenalin surge, wiping out the pain in my hip and all my other aches. Somewhere in the far distance of my mind I heard Tommy's voice, loud and clear. "I'm calling your number, Big Guy. Don't let me down."

The chain caught me on the forearm, sending a searing pain up to my shoulder. But the chain wrapped around my arm close enough to my right hand that I could grab the links.

I dropped the shield, yanked the bicycle chain forward and pulled Hat Man off balance. With all the strength I had left, I rammed his face into a support post. The impact shattered his nose and sent a gusher of blood from his smashed beak to his shirtfront. He howled in pain and sank to his knees, clutching at the torn flesh.

"This is for Motorcycle Mike and his Florida Gators," I said and kicked Hat Man in the side of the head. My Colorado hiking boots had the impact of a baseball bat. He fell over in a heap.

I whirled around and faced the other twin. His eyes bulged out of his head and spittle collected in the corners of his mouth. He had an odd black streak through his blond hair. He tightened his grip around Skylar's throat. "You take one more step and I'll break the little bitch's neck."

"If you hurt her, you're a dead man. I swear to God." Susan's voice cut through the tension in the store.

Everybody froze.

My daughter leveled her .38 Special at The Streak. It was the same gun she and I had argued over for years. Me contending no one needed a loaded gun in a civilized society and Susan beating me over the head with the 2nd Amendment.

The Streak eyed the gun and licked his lips. Indecision filled his face.

"Let her go." Susan's hand trembled, but at that distance, with all the gun training Susan had, there was no doubt she could hit The Streak. "Let her go now. I mean it."

The Streak weighed the situation. If he let Skylar go, he would lose his ace in the hole. Plus, there was a good chance Susan would shoot him anyway. He was right on that count. I knew my daughter and the look on her face told me the minute The Streak let Skylar go, Susan would blow him to Kingdom Come.

I didn't stop to think. I acted. I moved across the store as fast as I could. On the way, I grabbed the golf club off the coffin.

"Don't take another step," The Streak said, tightening his choke hold on Skylar's throat.

Skylar bent forward and sank her teeth deep into The Streak's bare forearm. He screamed and jerked his arm away. Skylar lunged to the side and I raised the nine-iron over my head and charged. I delivered a powerful blow to The Streak's shoulder with the head of the club.

The Streak whirled around and took a couple of staggering steps toward the back of the store. As he retreated, I brought the golf club down on his skull, sending him tumbling to the floor.

I swung the nine-iron back over my head and steadied myself to deliver another rage-induced blow to the man's head.

Behind me I heard a frantic clicking sound. Susan's gun was empty.

A maniacal laugh pierced the Halloween store.

I whirled around in time to see Hat Man fumble in the pocket of his field jacket and produce a gun of his own. From where I stood, it looked like a Glock and it looked deadly as hell.

Blood streamed down Hat Man's face. He leveled the Glock at my head and pulled the trigger.

And missed.

The bullet whizzed past my face and struck the wall behind me. The gunfire sounded like the explosion of a cannon in the confines of the Halloween store.

Hat Man had fired the gun one handed without using his other had to steady the weapon and the kick of the pistol had sent the bullet high.

A look of rage and frustration crossed his face. He aimed the gun again.

Suddenly, Jackie appeared from behind the shelf. She was holding what looked like a double-edged Viking axe. She reached the coffin in a couple of quick steps and slugged Hat Man in the face with the axe. The hard rubber snapped his head back.

Jackie belted him again.

Hat Man seized Jackie's arm and tried to hit her with the gun but she ducked under the punch.

She grabbed his arm, stuck out her foot, pulled him over her hip and flipped him on the ground. He landed hard on his back and the wind whooshed out of him. As he struggled to get up, Jackie slammed her palm into his already broken nose. Hat Man howled in anguish and the Glock fell out of his hand.

I hobbled across the room and threatened him with the golf club, but the second blow to his nose had taken all the fight of out Hat Man. He lay whimpering on the floor, clutching his damaged face.

"Where did you learn to do that?" I looked at Jackie with admiration.

Jackie grinned. "A guy I work with used to be a high school wrestler. He taught me a few moves. They came in handy on the job."

I shook my head. "I bet."

Suddenly, Hat Man's high-pitched laugh pierced the silence of the store. "I remember you," he yelled at Jackie. "Out at that dive on the highway. The porker with the saggy jugs."

Jackie's face turned red.

I whirled around and grabbed the edge of a shelf that was filled with Zombie Hunter costumes, Soul Taker gear and vampire outfits and toppled it over. The shelf and all the goods crashed down on Hat Man. He screamed in pain as a heavy box caught him square on his broken nose.

"That's no way to talk to a lady," I said. "Especially one that just kicked your ass."

Hat Man tried to glare at me, but the fight had totally gone out of him.

Skylar bounded over to us. "Bugs. Bugs. You saved us." She threw her arms around me. "You and. . ." She looked at Jackie.

"Skylar. Meet Jackie. I wouldn't have made it here without her."

Skylar let go of me and embraced Jackie. "Thank you. Thank you," Skylar sobbed.

Jackie looked startled at the impromptu hug. Then she looked pleased and comforted my granddaughter with a couple of pats on the shoulder.

Rand scrambled to his feet, crossed the room and threw his arms around me. I hugged him back. “You kicked ass, Bugs.” He turned and looked at Jackie. “You too,” he said with a grin.

Jackie smiled. “Thank you.”

“I’m not done yet,” I said. “How’s your head?”

“It seems okay,” Rand said. “For a while everything was foggy, but I think I feel okay now.”

“Good to hear,” I said. “But we’ll have to get you checked out for a concussion.”

Rand gave me a thumbs up.

I turned to Susan. “Are you okay?”

“I will be in a minute.” Susan’s voice was raspy. Tears filled her eyes. “Oh, Daddy. They were going to kill all of us. I forgot the bullets. It was so stupid of me. I was helpless. I didn’t have any control. Thank God you came.”

I sat down on the coffin and put my arms around my daughter. She buried her face in my shoulder and cried. I didn’t need to say anything. Holding her was enough. I loved her and she loved me. We had survived the worst together. That was what families did.

When Susan stopped crying, I looked across the store at Jackie, who was binding Hat Man’s hands behind his back with strands of rope from one of the Halloween hanging displays. She had already bound the creep’s feet.

I limped across the room and helped myself to some of the rope. “I’ll take care of the other one,” I said.

Jackie nodded.

The Streak was out cold. His face was matted with blood and his car had a bad cut that needed stitches. I bound his feet with rope and then tied his hands behind his back.

I helped Susan to her feet, introduced her to Jackie and rounded up the kids. The five of us headed for the store exit. Between my hip, Rand's possible concussion and Susan's ankle, it was a slow parade.

I pushed my way through what remained of the narrow front entrance of the Halloween store and stepped out onto the second floor of the mall and immediately knew in my gut that something was bad wrong.

CHAPTER 49

OUTSIDE THE STORE, THE LAST dying rays of the sun peeked through the enormous hole that had once been the roof of the Emerald Fields Mall, casting irregular shadows over the storefronts on the second floor.

Our ragged little band slowly made our way toward the escalator, which would lead us to the main floor.

"What will happen to those awful men we left in the Halloween store?" Skylar asked.

"We'll tell the authorities what those two bastards did and where they are and let the people in charge take care of them," I said.

I waited for Susan to spout her usual "language, Dad" comment but she just looked at me and smiled. "I hope the sonsofbitches rot," she said.

"Okay by me," Jackie added.

"You made a citizen's arrest, huh, Bugs?" Rand said with a big grin.

"You got it. Only I think we all made a citizen's arrest. I couldn't have done it by myself."

"Alright!!!" Rand and Skylar exchanged high fives.

"Let's get going," I said. "I'm guessing the National Guard is starting to land helicopters somewhere on the peninsula. Rescue teams can't be too far behind."

We took a couple of steps forward and suddenly my premonition about something being bad wrong turned into reality. The floor began swaying and groaning, the sound of metal against metal becoming deafening.

"What in the hell is that?" Susan frantically looked around her.

"The under structure is giving way!" Rand said. "All the girders and supporters are splitting and falling off. Listen. You can hear them hitting the bottom floor."

I listened and Rand was right.

The floor lurched downward and everyone scrambled to keep their balance.

"If we can make it to the escalator I think we'll be okay," I said. "We just need to get down to the bottom floor. Let's move as fast as we can."

That wasn't very fast.

Before we could get there, the escalator sank several feet, giving off its own groaning sound. Part of the floor in front of us caved in and crashed to the floor below, leaving a canyon, several feet across, between us and the escalator.

"We're trapped!" Susan's hand went to mouth. "We can't get down to the ground floor. We're stuck up here."

"Until the whole second floor collapses," Rand said.

I shot him a please-don't-say-anymore look.

"Maybe we could jump across that hole and still get to the escalator," Skylar said.

At the height of my football playing days there was no way I could have made the broad jump to the escalator, which was starting to sway and probably was going to collapse any second.

“Damn,” Jackie said.

“Amen to that,” Susan added.

“No. Wait,” Rand said. “I know an easier way to get to the ground floor.”

We all turned to look at him.

“No. Really,” Rand said. “I just thought of a way.”

“We’re listening,” I said.

“Over there,” Rand said. “Next to the Drug Rite. It’s Tech World. I go there all the time. They have all this cool electronic stuff.”

“So what?” Skylar snapped at her brother.

“I’m friends with one of the tech guys that works there. He’s a clerk. He told me one time that his girlfriend found out he was messing around with another girl. The girlfriend was furious and came up here looking for him. My friend was afraid she was going to come into the store and yell and scream at him and get him fired.”

“Sweetie,” Susan had far more patience than I had. “What’s the point of all of this?”

“My friend told me he snuck down the stairwell in the back of the store. The stairs lead to the ground floor and connect to the parking lot. The stairs are there because of some kind of fire code. I mean, I’ve never seen the staircase, but my friend said he used it to escape from his girlfriend.”

“Good thinking, partner,” I said and grinned at Rand. The kid had been cool under fire, not panicking and thinking of a reasonable way out of our dilemma. If he had a concussion, it probably wasn't a bad one.

The smile on Rand's face told me I hadn't compli mented him nearly enough over the years. But that was going to change immediately.

"What are we waiting for?" Jackie said.

We cautiously made our way across the swaying floor to the entrance of Tech World. Just as we reached the door, the escalator detached from his moorings and crashed to the floor below. The noise was deafening.

The electric sliding glass door that served as an entrance to Tech World was partially open so Susan and I took one side and Jackie and Rand grabbed the other side and we pried the doors open wide enough to let one person slip into the shop.

The interior of Tech World was dark but Rand knew his way around and led us to the back of the store. Using his shoulder, he pushed a door open and there it was.

A darkened stairwell.

We all gripped the handrail and stepping carefully, our little band inched our way down the stairs until we reached the ground floor. The door to the outside was locked but I'd come too far to let that stop me. I told everyone to get behind me and I delivered a sharp kick to the door bar.

Nothing happened.

I delivered another one. Still nothing. But on the third kick, the lock broke and the door swung open. And my hip rebelled with agonizing pain.

But we were in the parking lot.

Susan and I limped across the darkening field of asphalt, while Jackie and the kids followed us. As we got away from the mall, I turned and nodded to Jackie and she smiled back at me. Mission accomplished.

I threw my arm around Rand's shoulder and pulled him close to me. "Way to go, champ," I said. "Well done. You kept your head in a crisis and got us out of there."

Rand slipped his arm around my waist. "I learned from the best, Bugs."

CHAPTER 50

BISHOP RYAN HIGH SCHOOL WAS located a couple of blocks from the Zephyr Bay beach, a short walk from downtown Bay St. Edwards. Atlas had inflicted considerable damage to the school but the parking lot remained clear enough to serve as a helipad and the gym provided an ideal location for a hurricane survivor's shelter.

After escaping the Emerald Fields Mall, Jackie and Susan and the kids and I hiked down Florida Avenue. A few miles down the road, we got picked up by a state police SUV. The car had followed the National Guard troops and engineers over the morass of Highway 72. The Guard had partially reopened the highway for emergency vehicle traffic.

I was reluctant to even get in the state cop car at first, but I finally decided I was getting paranoid and I hopped in the front seat with the driver, a state police captain named Kennedy. Susan and Jackie and the kids scrambled into the back.

Captain Kennedy was a tanned fit-looking man in his late forties. He had neatly trimmed salt and pepper hair and wore an official state police blue windbreaker and tan slacks. He seemed like a nice guy. The SUV took us to Bishop Ryan.

I told Kennedy about the twins we had left tied up at the mall and told him about finding Mike's body in the motorcycle shop and about the dead couple at the Dragon Hill mansion. Susan piped up from the back seat and told Kennedy what she had witnessed on the beach in front of the Cromwell mansion. Then I told him about Officer Rollins and Cholo.

When we finished, Kennedy let out a low whistle. "We'll take care of it," he said in a voice that left no doubt that he would.

When we arrived at the Bishop Ryan gym, we found more officials and rescue workers than fellow survivors. A team from FEMA had filled a corner of the gym with cots and blankets. They had set up a folding table with hot coffee, sandwiches, cookies and bottled water. All of which were welcome.

A doctor and a pair of nurses had pitched a medical tent at the opposite end of the gym and the National Guard had hooked up a series of generators and the lights in the gym beamed down on us. Captain Kennedy and a couple of officials from the governor's office had appropriated the school's administrative offices to serve as a shelter headquarters.

At first, I wandered around the gym in a trance. My mind couldn't accept everything that had happened and it was hard to grasp that the nightmare was really over. Hurricane Atlas. The frantic search for Rand and Skylar. The fight with the psycho twins. It was all over. I needed to evaluate what I had left and look to the future, but for a while my brain insisted on replaying what I had happened over the last couple of days.

I peeked into the medical tent in the corner. A doctor in a white coat was examining Annie, the woman I had met briefly under the viaduct. She didn't look so good. Her skin was pale and her eyes looked vacant.

In the center of the tent, a masked doctor was working on some poor guy's face. The face was horribly swollen and blood flowed from several deep gashes. He must have been heavily sedated because the doctor was pushing and probing the swollen face with a variety of sharp instruments. I had to look away.

Bobby Joe sat on a cot by himself. He saw me in the entrance to the tent and waved. I waved back. That brought a little smile to his face.

A few minutes later, I got tired of walking around and sat down in the bleachers, rested my elbows on my knees and tried to come to grips with the massive upheaval that had been the latest chapter in my life.

"What did the doctor say about Rand?" Skylar said. She and I sat alone in the bleachers, watching the beehive of activity on the gym floor below.

"Your brother suffered a mild concussion," I said. "They're going to keep him in the medical tent overnight so they can keep an eye on him. He should be good as new in a day or two."

"That was pretty cool how he remembered the back stairs in Tech World," Skylar said. "I was so scared I could hardly think."

"Me too. I was really proud of your brother," I said. "Otherwise, I don't know what might have happened to us."

Skylar nodded.

I took a deep swig of coffee from a Styrofoam cup. "I was super proud of you, too. You did a great job of keeping everything together while you guys were trapped in the store."

“Thanks.” Skylar blushed. “How bad is Mom hurt?”

“Not as bad as it looks. She’s got a badly sprained ankle but the doctor doesn’t think it’s broken. She’ll have to stay off of it for a few days.”

Skylar sipped a soft drink from a can.

“You’ll have to pitch in and help out,” I said. “Your mother and your brother are going to need you.”

“I’m on it.” I could tell my granddaughter was enjoying her new, grown-up role.

“Will you and Mom go back to fighting when she gets better?” Skylar stared out over the gym floor.

I smiled. “I don’t think so,” I said. “At least I hope not. Living through a hurricane changes the way you look at things. You don’t take anything for granted. You change your perspective.”

“Like what’s important and what’s not?”

“Exactly.”

“Then at least something good will come out of the hurricane. You and Mom can be friends.”

“I’d like that,” I said.

Skylar sipped her drink. “When can we go home?”

“Not for a couple of days,” I said. “There’s a chance your house flooded. If that’s the case, we’ll have to find you guys somewhere else to live for a while. These people will help us.” I indicated the FEMA officials hustling around the gym floor.

A flurry of activity by the entrance to the gym pulled my attention away for a minute. We were too far away to hear what people were saying, but it looked like a camera crew from some TV station had arrived and wanted to come into the gym. A couple of state cops were shaking their heads no.

The TV people barreled past them.

The leader appeared to be an attractive, dark-haired woman carrying a clipboard. A nice looking, well-dressed man and a bevy of camera-toting guys trailed behind. The young woman gestured at the interior of the gym, while she talked to a FEMA representative. My guess was the crew wanted to come and do TV interviews with the hurricane survivors. Maybe get a couple of them to break down in tears. Must see TV.

"That's Ned Wallace. The TV weather guy," Skylar said. "He's a like a big celebrity on the Emerald Coast." She pointed to the man standing behind the woman with the clipboard. His teeth were blindingly white and he wore the ugliest checkered sport coat I had ever seen. A kid with an open laptop followed the woman with the clipboard around like a faithful dog.

In a minute, Captain Kennedy, the state cop who rescued us, came over and spoke to the TV people. He vigorously shook his head no and pointed to the door. The woman argued with him, but Kennedy held firm. He was not going to let the TV crew into the gym.

I was glad. The reporter would no doubt ask the dazed survivors stupid questions like "how does it feel to see your home totally destroyed?" Or "Were you scared when the hurricane hit?"

Ned Wallace tried to argue with Kennedy, but the state cop pointed to the door and shook his head no. Then he walked the TV people out of the gym.

I wanted to stand up and applaud.

CHAPTER 51

WHEN THE TV PEOPLE WERE gone, Skylar whipped out her cellphone. "The phones are working again," she said.

"Oh, thank God." It came out more sarcastic than I intended, which was my old-school, knee-jerk reaction to technology.

"Come on, Bugs. Just because when you were a kid, you guys had to use two tin cans and a string if you wanted to talk to someone."

"Very funny."

Skylar grinned. She punched and swiped on her phone for a while. I left her alone. It was her world.

I watched three new storm survivors stagger through the gym door. The FEMA people rushed to help them. One of the newcomers had a bloody, makeshift bandage wrapped around his head. He looked like a war casualty. The FEMA officials steered him over to the medical tent.

Skylar started to put away her phone.

"Hey," I said. "Can you show me how to do something on the cellphone? I heard they can do this, but I don't have a clue how to make it work."

"What is it?"

I told her.

"No problem. That's easy."

So is brain surgery if you know how to do it.

She held up her phone and gave me an impromptu lesson.

"Thanks kid, you're alright." It sounded like a line from a movie.

We watched the newcomers settle into the shelter.

"I like your new friend," Skylar said, putting away her phone.

"Me too."

"Jackie's really cool. She told me she had been through tough times when she was younger. She said you gotta always remember that no matter how bad you feel, the feeling won't last forever. That really helped me."

"She's pretty amazing."

"She told me she was going to college when things get back to normal. She said it doesn't matter how old you are, you're never too old to learn."

"A lotta wisdom there," I said, thinking about my own situation.

"Are you guys gonna hang out when all this hurricane stuff is over?"

"Me and Jackie?"

"Sure. You two seem to really get along."

I couldn't stop a grin from spreading across my face. "We'll see," I said. I tried to sound gruff but I couldn't pull it off.

Skylar grinned.

I pulled out the cellphone I had picked up at the Dragon Hill mansion and tried what Skylar and taught me. It worked like a charm. Never too old to learn. It was a good thing because I had an uneasy feeling the nightmare wasn't quite over.

AFTER A WHILE, SKYLAR LEFT and suddenly Susan was sitting beside me.

"Hey, Button," I said, using a nickname I hadn't used since Susan was in grade school.

Susan laughed. "Hey, Dad."

We sat in silence for a couple of minutes.

"Dad," Susan said in a halting voice.

"Yeah?"

"I think the hurricane was a wakeup call," Susan looked out over the gym floor. "I think it's time for me to be a better person. A better mother. Maybe even a better daughter." She snuck in a quick glance at me.

I let out a sigh. "Maybe it's time for me to be a better father," I said.

"You know, actually, you were pretty amazing in the mall," Susan said. "I mean, you came after us and fought with those creeps and you know, saved the day."

"I'll always have your back," I said, still watching the people milling about on the gym floor. "Yours and Rand's and Skylar's. Always. No matter what."

Susan draped her arm around my waist and rested her head on my shoulder. "I'm a lucky woman to have you for my dad."

"And I'm a lucky man to have such a wonderful daughter. Pretty. Successful. Smart. I think I sorta forgot that for a while."

“I think we both forgot some things,” Susan said, squeezing my shoulder. “But surviving the hurricane made me remember. Made me remember how much I love you.” She took a deep breath and exhaled. “You think we can make peace and start over.”

“No question,” I said. “I think we’re gonna need each other in the days ahead.”

“Then please know I’m here.”

“Back at you.”

Susan did her best to hold back her sniffles, but they came anyway. The real tears followed. I slipped my arm around her waist and hugged her. She would always be my little girl and the prospect of facing the next phase of my life with Susan and the kids securely in it was exciting.

We just sat together in the bleacher for a long time. No need for words. Just a father and his daughter.

CHAPTER 52

HOPING TO STRETCH MY SORE leg, I wandered out to the foyer of the gym, where I stopped to look at a giant wooden trophy case. The Bishop Ryan Rockets had won the state AA basketball championship a couple of years back. They had won state in football in 1998. I looked at the team pictures. The kids looked serious for the camera. Football and basketball mattered a lot when you were seventeen.

I envied the young men in the photographs. When those pictures had been taken the whole road stretched out in front of them. All the adventures. All the excitement. All the fun. All the heartache. All the life they could cram in. I hoped they embraced every minute of it.

The rescue team had provided some boxes of clothes in the gym and I selected a green windbreaker. It was a little snug, but who cared? I pulled out my phone and sent a quick text message, stuffed the phone in the pocket of the windbreaker and wandered around the gym some more.

When I circled around by the glass door that led to the parking lot, the bad news I'd been expecting was waiting for me.

"You need to come with me, sir." Police Chief Brunson leaned against the wall. His uniform was rumpled and stained and wet sand clung to his shoes and pants cuffs. His eyes were bloodshot and he needed a shave.

"Am I under arrest?"

"Something like that."

I nodded.

"You need to come now," Brunson said.

"And if I refuse?"

The chief put his hand on the pistol in the holster on his hip. "You don't have a choice," he said. "Resisting arrest is serious business. You don't want to find out how serious."

I shrugged.

Outside Bishop Ryan, early evening had descended on Bay St. Edwards. Shadows fell over the parking lot and the dunes beyond. The air felt damp and heavy and the salty smell of the Gulf was especially strong.

"Let's take a walk." Brunson pointed to a planked walkway that led away from the school toward the Zephyr Bay beach. I shrugged again. This was pretty much what I had been expecting. Jackie and I had witnessed a crime and I figured Chief Brunson would show up sooner or later.

The chief and I negotiated the walkway in silence, our feet crunching on the sand on the boardwalk.

I'd been through a lot in the last forty-eight hours and my body had used up its quota of adrenalin. All I felt was tired. But not too tired to know that I was in real danger.

A block down the walkway, we cut between a pair of tall dunes and stood on the edge of the beach. The waters had calmed and the tide appeared normal. The white sand had turned a dirty brown color.

"What'd you want?" I turned around and faced Brunson. He glared at me with cold eyes.

"I got some loose ends to tie up," the chief said.

"Why is that any concern of mine?" I jammed my hands into the pocket of my windbreaker.

"Because I saw you on the beach. Twice. Poking your nose in where it didn't belong."

"Maybe you shouldn't have been doing what you were doing," I said. "Maybe you should have been helping victims of the hurricane. Or is that not in your job description?"

Brunson let the comment go. "I know you were with somebody the second time you were spying on us, but I didn't get a look at them. I need to know who was with you."

"What were you doing on the beach?"

"Police business." The chief took a deep breath and hiked up his sagging trouser.

"You were burning corpses," I said. "Which is a strange activity under the circumstances."

"It was a matter of priorities. Now, who was with you?"

"Does the name Cholo mean anything to you?"

Chief Brunson bit down on his lower lip. The name had been like a kick in the gut. "Where'd you get that name?"

"I'm new to the coast but I heard this Cholo guy was a big pain in a lot of people's ass."

Brunson licked his lips. "Yeah. He was a Cuban guy. Did nothing but stir up trouble. Higher wages, better working conditions. All that crap. The guy was starting to hurt the tourist trade. That's where most people make their dough around here."

"What happened to him?"

"He moved on. End of story."

"That's not what patrolman Rollins told me. He said you and your cops murdered Cholo and his men and were trying to hide the evidence."

All the blood drained from Brunson's face. "You're out of line, Mr. Coffman. Way out of line. All of this is none of your business. Listen to me. I got better things to do than stand around out here and shoot the breeze with an old fart like you."

It surprised me that the chief knew my name.

"Now, for the last time, who was with you when you saw my guys on the beach?"

He wasn't going to get Jackie's name out of me no matter what. "So you admit burning the bodies on the beach had something to do with Cholo."

The look in Brunson's eyes told me I'd pushed things too far. He released the strap on his holster and pulled his gun. He did a quick survey of the deserted beach and then aimed the gun at my head.

I took a halting step backward.

"You got one more chance, Grandpa," the chief said, pushing the gun closer to my face. "Who was with you on the beach?"

CHAPTER 53

MY MILITARY TRAINING HAD BEEN years ago, but bits and pieces of what the army had taught me flashed through my mind.

If you are captured: Don't beg. Keep your dignity. That makes it harder to harm you. Don't insult or threaten.

Over Brunson's shoulder, I watched a gull dive into the bay.

You're probably going to die, so go for it. Put your hands up in the air in the "I surrender" position. It puts your hands close to the weapon.

I raised my hands and looked Brunson in the eye with a look that said "I'm not afraid of you."

Grab the gun barrel, twist it back and break their finger in the trigger hole.

"Who was it?" Brunson stepped closer and gestured with the gun.

Know your opponent. . . I couldn't remember what came after that.

"I figured I'd see you again," I said. "Obviously, I saw something on the beach I wasn't supposed to see. My guess is the hurricane uncovered some bodies you didn't think would ever turn up. I'm going out on a limb and assume Cholo was one of those bodies."

"I told you. The bastard moved on."

"Hurricanes change everything," I said. "Especially a man's perception. They also reveal his secrets."

"Cholo and his whole crew got what was coming to them. We don't need their kind around here. We don't need rabble-rousers. This is a peaceful place."

"And you and your men made sure it would stay that way."

"Damn straight."

The gull made another dive into the bay. This time he came up with a fish in his beak. He looked pleased with himself.

Brunson shoved the barrel of the gun an inch from my nose. "Who was with you? I want their name."

I shrugged again. "Sadly, we don't always get what we want," I said. "At this moment though, like the song says, I'm hoping like hell to get what I need," I said. This was the biggest gamble of my life. "I want you to meet my new friend, Captain Kennedy of the Florida State Police." I held my breath.

Brunson looked confused.

The gull circled the beach, showing off his catch.

Captain Kennedy stepped out from behind the dunes. He leveled his service revolver at Brunson. "Put down the gun, Chief," Kennedy said. "It won't do you any good now."

A pair of uniformed state troopers with their guns drawn appeared from behind the sandbank.

"How in the hell. . .?" Brunson shot me a look of pure hate and then lowered his gun.

"Drop it," Kennedy said.

Brunson's pistol made a soft thud in the damp sand.

I exhaled. "It's the 21st century, Chief," I said. "Earlier I told Captain Kennedy that I was on the beach. I told him I was expecting to see you again. When I spotted your patrol car in the Bishop Ryan parking lot, I sent my new friend a quick text message. Told him you were in the neighborhood."

"And I followed you two down here," Kennedy said. "Interesting conversation."

"Nothing you can prove," Brunson said with a smirk.

"Maybe we can," I said. "My granddaughter showed me a cool thing the cellphone can do. It can record. Is that great or what?" I pulled the phone out of my jacket pocket and held it up. "Will wonders ever cease?"

Captain Kennedy beamed. "Nice going."

The patrolmen moved quickly and handcuffed Brunson's hands behind his back.

Kennedy looked at me. "Damn," he said. "You are one gutsy old geezer."

I smiled. "You just gotta go with the flow," I said. "Technology is the world we live in. You gotta keep up with things." It was really hard to say that with a straight face, but I managed.

THERE WAS AT LEAST AN hour of daylight left and, on the walk back to Bishop Ryan, I heard the hum of chain saws and the rhythmic pounding of hammers in the distance. Apparently, a few optimistic souls were already starting to clear away debris and repair damaged ›mes. I admired their spirit.

Jackie sat by herself on the front steps on Bishop Ryan. She had cleaned up, found a pair of fresh jeans and a white over shirt in the FEMA bin. She stood up when she saw me. She looked beautiful in the fading daylight.

“Where you been, partner? I was worried about you. Susan said you headed off somewhere.”

“Had to tie up a loose end,” I said. “Sit down and I’ll tell you all about it. Turns out your intel on Cholo was right on the money. Officer Rollins wasn’t lying to us. He gave us the real story.”

We sat side by side on the steps, watching the sun slowly sink into the horizon beyond the bay. The crickets and cicadas started their evening symphony and I told her about Brunson and Captain Kennedy.

“Those poor Cuban guys. They were just trying to make a better life for themselves and others. What a sad thing.”

“Kennedy assured me the state authorities would launch a full investigation into what Brunson and his men did. I have no doubt there’ll be justice for Cholo and the others. It’s the least we can do for them as Americans.”

“I’ll drink to that,” Jackie said.

We sat in silence for a while. It was a comfortable quiet, the kind of quiet that two friends can share.

“I think your grandkids are terrific,” Jackie said after a while. “That Skylar is gonna be something. She’s already thinking about getting back to school and seeing her friends and getting on the soccer field.”

“It’ll be a while,” I said.

"But it'll happen. People in the gym are already talking about rebuilding Bay St. Edwards."

"I wish 'em well."

"I called Crystal City," Jackie said. "Talked to a friend of mine who lives across the hall from my apartment. She said our building only sustained minor damage. As soon as the power gets turned on, we're good to go."

That meant Jackie would head back up to Crystal City and her life would go back to normal. I was left with a sudden and crushing sense of regret.

"What are you going to do? I mean your house is gone."

I let out a deep sigh. "Yeah. I've been putting off thinking about that. Living with Susan would be pushing things. I don't think I'm ready for something like that."

Jackie looked down at her shoes and drew in a deep breath. "I've got another idea. Why don't you come with me to Crystal City. Stay at my place. I've got two bedrooms. You're welcome to stay there until you figure something out."

Could Jackie be serious?

"I'm just saying, you know. You're a lot of fun. Hurricanes. Rogue cops. Burning corpses, severed hands, psycho killers. What more could a girl ask?"

Jackie was serious about sharing her place.

"Besides, I could use your help to get going at the community college. I'm a little nervous about that. I mean a woman my age going back to school with all those smart kids is pretty daunting."

"They're not nearly as smart as they think they are," I said. 'ieve me, you know a whole lot more than they do."

Jackie smiled. "And you could give me some direction on my reading."

I grinned back at her. "Once a teacher, always a teacher," I said and felt an enormous sense of relief.

"If you come up to Crystal City with me we'd be just up the road from Bay St. Edwards and Susan and the kids."

"That would be perfect," I said. "The more I think about it, moving to Crystal City sounds like a plan. I think I'd like that. I think I'd like that a lot."

"Good. Then it's settled." Jackie took my hand and we exchanged squeezes, both of us excited about the future. Maybe she was right. Maybe the hurricane really might be a catalyst for a new life. Jackie rested her head on my shoulder and we watched the evening arrive while we listened to the crickets and cicadas.